Fellow Mortals & Other Stories by AM Burrage

Alfred McLelland Burrage was born in Hillingdon, Middlesex on 1st July, 1889. His father and uncle were both writers, primarily of boy's fiction, and by age 16 AM Burrage had joined them. The young man had ambitions to write for the adult market too. The money was better and so was his writing.

From 1890 to 1914, prior to the mainstream appeal of cinema and radio the printed word, mainly in magazines, was the foremost mass entertainment. AM Burrage quickly became a master of the market publishing his stories regularly across a number of publications.

By the start of the Great War Burrage was well established but in 1916 he was conscripted to fight on the Western Front. He continued to write during these years documenting his experiences in the classic book War is War by Ex-Private X.

For the remainder of his life Burrage was rarely printed in book form but continued to write and be published on a prodigious scale in magazines and newspapers. In this volume we concentrate on his supernatural stories which are, by common consent, some of the best ever written. Succinct yet full of character each reveals a twist and a flavour that is unsettling.....sometimes menacing....always disturbing.

There are many other volumes available in this series together with a number of audiobooks. All are available from iTunes, Amazon and other fine digital stores.

Table Of Contents

Fellow Mortals

And just because I was thrice as old
And our paths in the world diverged so wide,
Each was naught to each, must I be told?
We were fellow mortals, naught beside?
'Evelyn Hope'—Robert Browning

The odd thing was that her name was Evelyn Hope. Poets of the Chestertonian school may know a great deal about village innkeepers, and what village innkeepers sell, but the village innkeeper does not often respond to buying the poet's wares or acquainting himself with them. But twenty years or so before this story really begins, when Dick Hope—'Good old Dick Hope', who kept The Sun, at Bringfield—became the father of a daughter, some passing stranger informed him over the morning glass that a famous poet had written a poem about 'beautiful Evelyn Hope'.

Dick's imagination seized upon this, and he had the child baptised Evelyn, not knowing whether she would grow up to be beautiful, but hoping for the best. It was not until afterwards that he bought, second-hand, a copy of the poems and discovered that the only one in which he was interested began with the ill-omened words: 'Beautiful Evelyn Hope is dead'.

Well, this Evelyn Hope, daughter of Dick, was also beautiful, and, if we are to trust the registrar, she is also dead. But is she? Does all that remains of this lovely child lie under a long green hump in Bringfield churchyard? I don't think so. I don't believe in ghost stories when they are told me by wild-eyed, long-haired young men with clammy hands. But when you get them from the hard-bitten business man they command respect.

There is a type of men, not very uncommon, to be seen at fashionable seaside hotels at weekends. They are generally to be found under a palm in the winter garden, smoking a very good cigar and with costly refreshment at the elbow. They are generally between fifty and sixty, very well dressed in light grey, obviously not quite gentlemen, but doing their best, and giving the impression that for the past quarter of a century they have been doing themselves a little too well. If you see one of these and have with you a friend who is in the know, you will get an elbow in the ribs and a whisper in the ear saying: 'You know who that is, don't you? So-and-so, the great financier.'

Of such is Arthur Holbeck, director of I forget how many companies. Now, I would not trust Mr So-and-so, the great financier, if he advised me to invest my few pennies. I am cynical enough to suspect the ulterior motive. I do not know that I should trust Mr Arthur Holbeck, who had owned to having deviated a little from the straight and narrow way. But when Mr Arthur Holbeck, who belongs to a type which is generally ashamed to profess a belief in God, the after-life, or anything more mystical than a sausage, shrinkingly and confidentially tells me of an occult experience, I am going to give it seventy-five per cent credence.

Here is his tale—in his own words.

You used to know Bringfield and good old Dick Hope who kept The Sun, and it's a pity you don't remember the kid. Still, it wasn't likely you'd have seen her unless you'd stayed in the place. In those days she must have been at the nearest secondary school for girls, one of those jabbering kids with attache cases that you see mornings and evenings swarming into buses and trains. I was fond of her, even in those days. There was something—what do you call it?—ethereal about her. She was an odd kid to have come out of a country pub.

Bringfield isn't the ideal village, but it's the nearest I've found to it so close to London. I found it, trying to get out of the weekend traffic on the road to Brighton. I pulled up at The Sun for a spot of lunch, and I was surprised at what a good lunch I got. They'd got a bottle or two of '06 Cliquot in the cellar, and one was drinking '06 in those days. And, again, what decent people the Hopes were. Always smiling and looking as if they were glad to see you for your own sake, instead of having both eyes on your money. The old-fashioned sort.

I suppose the man with a low taste for villages and village pubs has always got his favourite spot. Often, when I could spare the time, I was down at Bringfield, sometimes spending a night or two. The farmers, dealers, and labourers I used to meet in The Sun were all awfully good fellows and began to welcome me like an old friend. They were a change from the mob I herded with in the City and lunched and dined with most days of the week. When I was there I was always the most important person on hand. Well, I was used to that in very different spheres. But it tickled my vanity more there than elsewhere. The people, Hopes and all, may have had ulterior motives in making a fuss of me, but the motives weren't quite so ignoble as those of the fat well-to-do men elsewhere, who lushed me up in the hope of getting to know which way the cat was going to jump in the City. I didn't know any of the local gentry, and didn't want to, but two or three of the farmers had their own rough shoot, and I could always get a day's sport in the season when I wanted it, so I used to keep a gun at the inn. Bringfield became my second home. Most of us like to think that we enjoy the simple things of life. I honestly think I did. It was a delightful change to mix with simple people, talk simple talk, eat simple food, and drink beer.

Evelyn was only a child when I first knew her, with long plaits of yellow hair—so long that she wasn't allowed to be bobbed or shingled like other little girls. She might have stepped straight out of one of Hans Andersen's fairy tales. We took to each other at once—I forty and something, and she thirteen. I might have been her father or her uncle. I never had a kid of my own, and I never took to one as I took to her.

I'm not going to try to describe her. She was just a lovely little creature.

I'm not an imaginative man, but it always seemed to me that there was something about her that didn't quite belong to this world. Years later, when she was eighteen or so, I discovered what it was. There was a girl in a stained glass window in the parish church something like her, that seemed to have that air of hers. Some saint or other. I don't know who the girl in the stained glass window was supposed to be.

Not that there was anything saintly about Evelyn so far as you'd notice. She was just an ordinary jolly kid. I watched her grow up, through being down there off and on at weekends and for odd days. When she was seventeen or so, and old enough to help in the bar, she left school. Work in a bar, according to a well-meaning society and many private individuals, is supposed to be bad for a girl. I dare say it is in some cases, but it all depends on the girl. It didn't hurt Evelyn.

Most of the customers at The Sun were decent enough in their speech, but occasionally 'language' came floating across from the tap-room, particularly late in the evenings. The old scamps who didn't mean any harm and hardly knew when they were swearing. She heard it and yet didn't hear it, if you can understand me. She never turned and told them to shut up. Nasty words glanced off her mind like water off a duck's back.

Just before this time, in defiance of the wishes of her parents, she had her long hair cut, and what was left of it shingled and waved and all the rest. She wanted to look like other girls. I could have smacked her. She stopped looking like one of Hans Andersen's princesses, but she couldn't stop looking like the saint in the window.

You'll say that I idealised her, but I didn't. To idealise is to imagine perfection where it doesn't exist, and she was the perfect creature. You'll also stick your tongue in your cheek and guess what happened to my middle-aged heart and head, and you'll guess right—and wrong.

Thank Heaven I had a sense of the ridiculous and a sense of proportion.   When she was nineteen and I was fifty-two I was in love with her like any callow boy. But I saw that it had to begin and end with my being a sort of rich uncle. I could see myself in the glass, thank you! Is there anything in the world more ludicrous and unedifying than a middle-aged man running after a young girl? I saw myself slightly grey, rather too ruddy to be healthy, and with a paunch on me. No, it just couldn't be done. I'd laughed and sneered too often at other men for the same kind of folly.

Mind you, at that time, I think the kid would have married me. She was fond of me in the same way that I pretended to be fond of her. Dick Hope and his missus would have been delighted. I was no chicken, but they thought I was a millionaire. However, I had the sense to see that it wouldn't work. I wasn't going to appear as the corpulent middle-aged lover with his purchased bride. I knew she couldn't love me as she might love some fresh-faced boy.

At about this time, as was only natural, a number of young men who 'just happened to be passing' began to drop in at The Sun. They were the sort of young men who wore brilliantly coloured scarves, Fair Isle jumpers, and plus fours, and rode too fast on motor-cycles. I knew them through and through, and why they came. I could tell what they were, how they lived, and guess to within a few shillings a week the salary that each of them earned. In more than one of them I recognised myself of thirty years ago.

Dick and his missus called her 'Evie' of course. They were the sort of people who would. Couldn't leave a beautiful name alone, but had to mutilate it as a term of endearment. I'm not running them down, because I was fond of them, but the kid was always Evelyn Hope to me.

My fondness for Evelyn and hers for me was quite an open thing, and this frankness put on the relationship a sunlight and fresh air which, in the eyes of spectators, made it appear that it was just what I pretended it was. Before an audience we used to call each other 'darling' and talk about our wedding-day, and all that. To the audience I was just the elderly, good-natured, wealthy man, buffooning with the girl of the inn. Everybody knew that I was fond of the kid, but even Dick Hope and his missus didn't guess that I was fond of her as some smooth-faced boy might have been fond of her.

That was my secret—and Evelyn's. How did she know? Oh, God knows how women of any age from three upwards learn secrets they haven't been told. And how did I know she knew? Well, that comes presently. Meanwhile, I kept it up, you see, with hollow laughter—the joke that I was Evelyn's sweetheart. And the fact that it was so readily accepted as a joke—even apparently by Evelyn herself—showed me what sort of ass I should have looked if I had meant it to appear anything else.

Well, as was only natural, one of the young men with motor-cycles became gradually more prominent than the others. He started taking Evelyn to the pictures and dances and all that.

He was a nice boy named Jack Hilling, who was in a bank in a mid-Sussex town. To him I appeared just as a benevolent old man who had to be spoken to respectfully not only on account of his supposed wealth and position, but also because of his advanced age.

I knew instinctively that he was the man whom Evelyn would choose out of the assortment that gathered round. I liked the boy. I honestly believe I wasn't jealous of him.

One glorious day in May I arrived at The Sun for a weekend. Everybody seemed radiant, and there was a sort of air about the place which you find when some pleasant secret is about to spread. Then it was whispered to me. Evelyn was engaged to Jack Hilling.

I opened a bottle, of course. I think I acted my part rather well as the sort of benevolent uncle who was delighted at the news and who could be relied upon to come down rather heavily in the matter of a wedding present. In fact, I don't know that I was acting. I had known that Evelyn would find her mate sooner or later so it was no shock—and I liked the boy.

It was when I privately congratulated Evelyn that she gave herself away; gave herself away, I mean, by letting me know that she knew what was in my heart, and letting me know too that she was very well aware that I was her man, kept from her by a paltry barrier of a few years out of eternity, but also by an inexorable law of nature.

I'd started some fumbling little speech of congratulation, when she smiled and gave me her fist like a man. While I held her hand I said it was about the nicest thing that could happen in this world—one of those fatuous, facile things that anyone might say. Then, to my surprise, her eyes filled. She leaned towards me, stood on tiptoe, and kissed me on the cheek—for the first time since she was a tiny kid.

'This world?' she said. 'Does it matter very much? I believe that all the things we want to happen and don't, have happened before—only we don't remember—and will happen again.'

I understood her. Of course, she'd read 'Evelyn Hope'. What girl, however much she might dislike poetry, wouldn't have read a poem about her own namesake. I was rather queerly happy. I remembered those lines:

'Delayed it may be for more lives yet,
Through worlds I shall travel not a few,
Much is to learn, much to forget,
Ere the time be come for taking you.'

I don't go in for poetry much myself, but I happened to know 'Evelyn Hope' for precisely the same reason that Evelyn herself knew it. Well, it was good to know that she realised what I did—that I was her man, and that in this life we'd been separated by a decade or two. Just missed each other, as it were. Meanwhile, it was a case of youth to youth. She was fond of Jack Hilling in a way that she couldn't be expected to be fond of me.

What was left for us both was to wait for our destined ends. Then, it amused me to think, I might wake up a few hundred years hence as a little Dutch baby, grow up, and fall in love with some little Dutch girl who would be another incarnation of Evelyn. Only—and here is the snag if these things really happen—we shouldn't remember anything or know that we'd once been Evelyn Hope and old Holbeck.

Well now, I can hurry on a bit. I had a houseboat at Laleham that summer, and gave the Hopes and young Hilling a standing invitation to come down for any weekend or part of a weekend when they could get away. My visitors were always a pretty mixed bag, and I was always independent. If any of my friends didn't like the Hopes, well, then, they could lump it. The Hopes never came, and one Saturday, faced with the prospect of a lonely weekend, I wired to Dick and invited him down for the Sunday. I got back a reply: 'Sorry cannot get away, but I am sending somebody you like'.

Well, I knew who that would be. Evelyn, of course. And she would be chaperoned by somebody, probably her fiance. He'd be bringing her on the pillion of his motor-bike. So I ordered the old girl who was looking after me to get some lobsters from Chertsey, and lay in the materials for a very special salad. And I spent half the Sunday morning making a hock-cup in my own way. And—they didn't turn up. I waited on board all day, and night fell, and still they didn't turn up.

Oh, well, without any sob-stuff I may as well tell you bluntly that they were both killed on the road—ran head-on into a lorry somewhere near Dorking.

I was stunned at first, but not as heart-broken as you'd think. If what I hoped were true she'd just gone first, and after I'd followed we'd meet again elsewhere.

Poor Dick Hope, her father, took it differently. It broke him up. He was dead by the end of the summer. The pub changed hands. Dick had made a bit of money, and his missus went to live in a boarding-house at Worthing. After that I chucked visiting Bringfield.

And now I'm coming to the queer part of my story.

My affairs were coming to a crisis. Things had gone pretty badly wrong. I've told you just this part of the story before. Very few people who've gambled as I have, with other people's money to help, have avoided sailing pretty near the wind. I won't bore you with the details, but I could see myself heading for an almighty crash.

I could see daylight at the other end of the tunnel, so to speak, but that tunnel was three months long, and to get over that three months I needed forty thousand pounds. The banks were hopeless. My securities were already pledged, and although a good many in the know saw the way I was heading, I was only going to hasten the crash if I publicly owned the mess I was in by trying to get money.

For a long while I had hopes about one man. His name was Curran. He could see a few months ahead the same as I could. I sounded him, but he didn't seem to respond, and that was the last straw.

Well, it wasn't just a case of going broke. There was a bit more in it than that, as I've owned. I don't want to excuse myself. You mustn't gamble with other people's money, even if you want to get them, besides yourself, out of a mess. There was a pretty nasty scandal, topped by Portland or Dartmoor, staring me in the face. I decide to fade out and try another world. For the previous few months I hadn't had much use for this one.

I wasn't afraid of death, but I was terrified of just the act of crossing the frontier. That nasty final moment. How should the thing be done, and where ought it to be done? I turned it all over in my mind for about three days. Then I thought of The Sun at Bringfield—now in other hands—where I kept a gun.

Just the gun, I thought, and a bit of string with a loop at the end, and the long trick would be over. Cowardly, of course, but better from my point of view than disgrace, scandal, Portland, and, subsequently, an old age spent in shame and penury. I'd go down for the weekend, and on the Monday morning I'd take the gun out into a field and—oh, well, you can guess. I went down all right, and I spent the Saturday evening and the Sunday in a state of forced hilarity. In the eyes of the world, and particularly of that village, I was a rich man. I treated everybody. I was the good fellow. When a man is short of forty thousand, a fiver or so doesn't matter much if he has it in his pockets.

The new people who had The Sun were Cockneys and rather servile. I was the rich man they'd heard about who'd adopted the village and used to come and stay in the house when the Hopes were there. I was the man who treated all the villagers and drank champagne.

Oh, yes, I was very welcome. I don't mind owning that I was fairly well primed when I went to bed on the Sunday night, which I thought was going to be the last night of my life. It would have been, but for the miracle I'm going to tell you about.

I'll indulge your scepticism with an admission or two. I'd had more than one drink, and it was the first time I'd stayed there since the Hopes had gone, so it wasn't unnatural that I should dream of Dick Hope.

I seemed to dream of him all through the night. He kept on coming in and out of dreams which I don't remember, until one dream became clear and extremely vivid. There was only Dick Hope in it, and nothing and nobody else. He looked at me very intently as if he knew all about me, and understood. And he said very distinctly: 'I am going to send somebody you like.'

Those, of course, were the words of his telegram, just before Evelyn was killed on the road. Not very strange, you say. Wait a minute.

After—I don't know how long after—I became slowly conscious and was distinctly aware of being slowly awakened. I mean that I wasn't waking spontaneously. Somebody—or something—outside myself was the cause. And then, still three-parts asleep, I began to discover what it was. There was something soft and warm on my cheek. I groped for it without opening my eyes, and it was a plait of hair.

Then I did open my eyes. It was just early twilight, and I could see quite clearly. Somebody who had been bending over me got up and withdrew a step or two. It was Evelyn.

Now you can say what you like about this, except just one thing. You may say that I was off my head and suffering from delusions, arguing that a man about to take his own life cannot be in his right state of mind. Although I think—and know—differently, I could not fairly quarrel with that criticism. But you mustn't say I was dreaming. I was as wide awake as I am now, and it was those two plaits of hair brushing my face that wakened me. She had stepped backwards four or five feet and now stood close to the window, the upper half of her framed by the glass through which filtered that bluish, morning twilight. And although, with what light there was coming from behind her, the face and figure turned towards me should have been in the shadow, I could see her as clearly as I now see you.

Oh, yes, she was Evelyn—Evelyn as a kid before she had had those yellow plaits of hers cut off. She was the Goose Girl in Hans Andersen again, and yet still the saint in the stained-glass window. There she stood, beautiful and radiant and smiling, and there was something about her—a kind of purity—which I can't describe.

I knew that I was awake, and while something beat and clamoured in my brain, telling me that Evelyn was dead, I had no fear of her whatever. Why, I was hardly in awe of the kid. I held out my arms to her. I was a lonely, unloved man, going to his death in an hour or two, and I wanted her to come and comfort me. But she shook her head without ceasing to smile, and only her eyes seemed to kiss me across the space between us. Then her lips moved.

I can't say that she actually spoke aloud. Really, you know, I can't be sure. Nor have I ever learned the art of lip-reading. Perhaps I felt rather than heard what she said. It was just two words: 'Curran—today'. She repeated them again, looking at me as if to ask if I understood. So then I nodded, and suddenly found myself staring at a rectangle of a window which framed nothing more than the growing twilight, and myself once more alone in the room.

I couldn't have been asleep, because I got up then and there and dressed.

You see this bit of string and the loop at the end? Well, I didn't use it, nor the gun in the landlord's parlour. When full daylight came I drove myself up to town and arrived at the office at the usual time.

It was a rotten morning. I had a bad time staving off importunate inquirers on the telephone, but I knew beyond all doubt that Curran—whom I had already given up in despair—was coming to the rescue. I was no surer that the sun would set that evening.

And he arrived at noon, and we went into figures for an hour and then went out to lunch together. He could see into the future just as well as I could, and he could also see that by saving me he could line his own pockets. Before the banks closed at half-past three I had his guarantee for £40,000.

Well, you know the rest. I just squeezed round the comer—thanks to Evelyn. I'm not a religious man or a superstitious man, but I know I shall meet her again somewhere else. And I'm pretty sure I shouldn't, if I'd used the gun and this little bit of string, and she knew it, too. That's why she came to me. The sad thing is that we shan't know each other, or remember, but that won't matter, once we've forgotten. It won't happen tomorrow, or the day after. 'Delayed it may be for more lives yet'. But I like to think, to believe, that some day I shall be a boy again, and that my boyhood will match her girlhood, whether we race on wild horses over the hills of Heaven or meet on this earth again as children of a race as yet perhaps unborn.

Meanwhile, whatever may happen to me in this world, I shall have no use for this (and he began to fold up very carefully the bit of string with a loop at the end), except as something to remind me of that early morning at The Sun.

I thought when I tied that little knot that all would end with just one twitch of the string. But I know now that—ah, well, you think I've been talking through my hat. Thanks at least for not laughing.

The Man on the Corner

Covers-Brosdale did not call himself a specialist, although there were several branches of the healing profession of which he could have claimed a specialist's knowledge. A specialist is, after all, only a man who has devoted most of his time to a narrow channel of study, shutting out as best he may all other distractions.

So Covers-Brosdale remained a G.P., and was known to all and sundry in his neighbourhood as 'a very clever doctor'.

Rival practitioners, well aware that his limitations equalled their own, called him in as a 'second opinion' when occasion demanded. They knew what he was going to say before he said it. But Covers-Brosdale had that gift of inspiring confidence which is eighty-five per cent of the art of healing.

'In the last hundred years,' he would say, 'surgery has advanced at very long strides, and medicine has stood still. There are about half a dozen drugs which have been found helpful. The rest is nothing.

'Get a patient's confidence, so that he will follow ordinary commonsense advice which anybody could give him, and nine times out of ten you have cured him.

'If the patient has a strong belief in medicine, let him have some, of course. The nastier the better. It is like a penance to a repentant sinner.

'Frighten a patient into mending his habits, and, at the same time, induce him to take a tablespoonful of "the mixture as before" after each meal. Then, Providence willing, you will have a cure, and he will attribute it to the prescription.'

So he did much good by auto-suggestion; and grateful patients sent him other patients in their turn. Still more came who were passed on to him by fellow doctors.

A doctor's business is to cure a patient, and in this unselfish profession it is not uncommon to pass him along to a fellow practitioner who may be able to 'talk him well'.

After waiting for half an hour on an April morning, Mr Leyden was shown into the consulting room. He was a heavily-built man in the early fifties, and he spoke in a cultured voice.

'Good morning. I wonder if you'd mind running the rule over me?'

'What's the trouble?'

'Well, I don't know. Like to know how I am in a general sort of way. I'd like you, if you don't mind, to treat me as if I'd been sent you by an insurance company. '

'Very well. Just take off your coat and waistcoat, will you?'

The examination took about five minutes. Then came the questions. All save one, and the answers they received, were unimportant.

'Ever had rheumatic fever?'

'No. But you mean my heart's wrong. Anything serious?'

'No, nothing organically wrong. A weakness. A little enlarged and dilated. Nothing to worry about. Good enough to last you for another thirty years or so. Don't smoke too much and don't drink tea that's been standing too long. That's all Yes, if I were representing an insurance company, I should accept you as a first-class life for a man of your age.'

Leyden looked relieved, then his face clouded again.

'Actually,' he said, 'I think my trouble is mental. Perhaps I should have gone to an alienist. But I heard about you and—well, here I am.'

'Yes? Well, what's the trouble?'

'Would you say that I am going off my head, or that I'm mad already?'

'So far, you have seemed reasonable enough. Why?'

'Because for years I have been suffering from what you would call an obsession or a fixed idea. '

The doctor smiled.

'You'd better tell me,' he said

The other drew a long breath.

'There's a man going about whom I feel sure is going to kill me.'

'Oh, what have you been doing to him?'

'Nothing. I don't know him. I've never even spoken to him. During the past thirty or so years I've seen him perhaps ten or eleven times, always when I least expect to.

'I always meet him suddenly at corners. I'm turning one way, and he's turning the other. I don't think he remembers having seen me before, but I know him. I know him only too well.'

'Anything sinister or in any way distinctive in his appearance?'

'Nothing. The last twice I've seen him, he's been getting rather grey. Round red face, and there's a cleft in his right eyebrow, as if he'd had a cut there at some time. He's generally carrying a leather case, and I think he's some kind of commercial traveller. That would account for my having seen him in so many different places.

'I begin to forget him—and sometimes almost do forget him for a bit—and then almost literally I bump into him again. Always at a corner—and that, in a sort of way, is where one meets sudden death. Always at a corner. '

'Well, his basilisk glare hasn't killed you yet, has it? And you may never see him again. And, if you do, you'll walk past each other as usual.'

'I can't get it out of my head that one of these days he'll speak to me, and, when he does speak to me, I shall die.'

The doctor smiled tolerantly.

'And that,' he said, 'is precisely what you've got to get out of your head. Of course, it's all absurd, and you can see the absurdity of it for yourself. Otherwise you wouldn't have mentioned it to me.

'You've got to think a bit of that heart of yours. The fewer worries you have, the better, you know. I suppose, like the rest of us, you've one or two real worries? Why trouble with those which don't really exist?'

'I know. It's all very absurd. I feel a fool for telling you. But there it is. If I meet him again, would you recommend me to speak to him? Just invent a sudden excuse. Then he'd answer me, and nothing would happen, and I should feel all right ever afterwards.'

The doctor considered, and shrugged his shoulders.

'No-o. I don't know that I recommend you to do that. It would cost you an effort. Besides, with that peculiar mental kink of yours it would prove nothing. You'd be saying to yourself: "Well, it'll be the *next* time we meet." And the next time you met he might wish you good morning, having remembered speaking to you before. And it would always be the next time.

'Just cut him out of your thoughts, and, if you ever see him again—and, of course, you never may—just pass him as you always have passed him. That's all. Meantime, don't think about him. I don't suppose you've ever told another what you've just told me?'

'No.'

'Well, you'll find that the mere fact of telling me has done you good. Confession is good for the soul, and what we call the soul is the mind, and the mind is controlled by the brain, which partly controls the body and is partly controlled by it.

'Go away in peace, and laugh at yourself, if you can. After all, you may not see him again. Incidentally, of course, he may be dead already.'

'No, he isn't dead.'

'How can you know, if you know nothing about him?'

'I feel I should know it if he were dead.'

The doctor frowned.

'That, of course, is imagination,' he said, 'and imagination is the source of most evils and a great deal of good. Just go in peace, and think you may never see him again. You never may. If you do, just laugh to yourself when you've passed him, and say: "Well, he let me off that time." It's all in your own hands. '

'You've met other cases like mine?'

'Yes—and no. No, because two cases are never precisely alike, any more than two colds in the head breed precisely the same number of germs. If the man had been an avowed enemy, or somebody that you were conscious of having wronged, the case would be different.'

He rose and named a very modest fee. The patient, who looked happier already, paid it.

The doctor moved towards the door, but turned suddenly.

'Come and see me again,' he said, 'after you have next encountered—er—your evil genius.' He paused and smiled at his own expression. 'I shan't charge you any fee. I shall be interested to hear if you have reacted in the same way—now that you have told me your trouble. Good morning. Don't forget.'

He went to the door, opened it, and so they parted. An hour later, after he had shut the door on the last of the morning's callers, he took a few notes. The fellow had been mildly interesting. But only mildly interesting.

Eleven weeks passed—or eleven weeks and two days, as his diary told him—and then came the sequel.

It was close on 11 o'clock one night, and he was just settling down to the last whisky and soda. The bell rang and he went to the door himself, for the servants were probably in bed.

On the upper step was a working man, evidently greatly agitated.

'Can you come at once, sir? Policeman sent me.'

'What's the matter?'

'Man dead, sir. At least, the policeman thinks he's dead. Told me to run and fetch the nearest doctor. Beg your pardon for troubling you, sir. '

'How did it happen? Been an accident?'

'I suppose it must have been a sort of accident.'

'Well, where is he?'

'Corner of Main-street and Grantham-street, sir. No distance.'

'All right. I'll come along with you. Just wait a minute.'

He had a first-aid case ready packed. He hurried into the surgery and fetched it. He set off at a pace which made the short-legged man beside him break into a clumsy trot.

The doctor smiled grimly to himself, knowing the type of man who had called him. Death and disaster were meat and drink to men of his sort, and even superseded racing and professional football as subjects for discussion. A football match is generally over by the following Wednesday, but the last moments and the later obsequies of an aunt are good for six months.

It was not far to go, and the ambulance had not yet arrived. The police were now four strong and had given up telling a gathered crowd to 'pass along, please'. The crowd, which could do nothing, stared and gaped, as crowds do. They loitered just to see what would happen next. So long as the body and the policemen were there, so long would the crowd remain.

Way was made for the doctor. At least, everybody at first stood firm and told everybody else to get out of the way. He pushed his way through and bent over the man who lay on the pavement.

On the instant he recognised him. Then he took him by the wrist, looked at the eyes, and hastily unfastened the shirt. Somebody had already undone the collar.

The doctor's face was expressionless. He looked up at one of the officers.

'Ambulance coming?' he asked.

'Yes, sir.'

'Very well. Mortuary. How did it happen?'

'This man can tell you, sir.'

The man referred to was already telling another policeman for about the tenth time.

'I don't know that I ever saw him before in my life. Just before I got to the corner I took out a cigarette. Found I hadn't got a match. Well, when you want a light, you always ask the next man who's smoking to give you one. Nothing in that, is there? Everybody who smokes has done the same thing hundreds of times. So I just stopped him, and asked him to give me a light.

'Well, directly I spoke, he gave me one awful look. I'll never forget that look. He went over just as if he'd been knocked down by a bullet. Crash! He went, and there he was on the pavement at my feet.'

The doctor looked at the man, and suppressed an inclination to breathe noisily. He was short and elderly, and the shock had not withdrawn all the colour from his florid face. One of his eyebrows had a cleft in it.

'It wasn't my fault, was it, sir?'

The doctor did not answer. There are some direct questions to which neither 'yes' nor 'no'

'Is quite the truthful reply.

'You didn't know the man?' he asked quietly.

'Never seen him before—not as I remember.'

'All right. You'll have to give evidence, though, I'm afraid. Don't worry. You won't be blamed.'

The ambulance arrived, the crowds split up into smaller crowds which loitered away. The doctor went home thoughtfully, and wrote something of interest to his own kind before he went to bed.

He did not perform the post-mortem, but he had to give evidence at the inquest. It was merely perfunctory evidence, and, if he suppressed something under oath, it may be forgiven him—for all we know.

Anyhow, he did not consider it good for the lay mind to know as much as he knew—and that was very little. At the best it would have done no good to the innocent cause of the disaster.

On the night after the inquest he sat alone in his study and smoked and thought; and what he thought will never be known, unless his private notes survive him.

The Sisters of Changton Margery

The other day my friend Bernard Hilldon punched the head of George Flake for calling him a liar. This, in our present state of civilisation, is highly regrettable. The civilised way of calling a man a liar is to cough, murmur something rapidly about something else, and leave his presence in a marked manner. You thus let him know what you think of him without quite giving him an excuse for hitting you. On both sides, I think, it was a very crude affair.

It happened through Bernard telling George Flake the story I am about to relate. It is possible that he stretched it a bit—I don't know, for I wasn't present—but it doesn't need any stretching. It is an experience which Bernard and I shared together five years ago come next October, and we don't want to share such another.

Bernard and I were juniors in the same firm, and you know what happens to juniors in the matter of holidays. They have to take their holidays outside the holiday season. We were told to take our fortnight in October. We didn't mind in the least; in fact we were rather glad. Our tastes were very similar. We didn't want to lie on our backs on the shingle of some tripper-haunted beach in August. We both liked walking, but there is not so much fun in walking when you are sweating and swallowing dust all the time.

October is a lovely month, with the red and yellow leaves above and on the ground. There is plenty of sun, for the weather is generally fine, and a nip in the air which lends a zest to taking exercise. There is very little chance of reaching a small place where you intend to stay the night and finding yourself crowded out. The people one encounters are pleased to see strangers and have more time to talk to them.

We began saving up for our holiday months in advance. Our intention was to cross France and walk in the Basque country. But you know how it is with very young men who are earning their own livings, and not very good livings at that. All sorts of unforeseen necessities made a run on the bank. One is always being compelled to buy shoes, socks, hats, and underclothes. Poor old Bernard had to make a series of painful and expensive visits to his dentist. And sometimes we couldn't resist the temptation to go up West for a dinner and a show.

Thus the holiday fund became so depleted that by September it might almost be said that we had an overdraft on it. For that year, at least, the Basques would be denied the honour of a visit from us. Foreign travel was out of the question. But there was England left. There is always England for the poor, thank God!

We argued about where we should go. We both loved the west and had no call to Wales or to the north. The east is inclined to become a little too bleak in October. We had 'done' Cornwall twice and Devon once. Devon would have borne a second visit, but it is no county for poor travellers. In Devon nowadays, or at the time of which I write, the innkeeper or any other lessor of lodgings stingeth like an adder. Gone are the days when you could walk into the humble wayside cottage and have tea, saffron cake, bread and butter, jam and cream, and the good housewife looked ashamed of charging you sixpence. Nowadays they wait for you very much in the spirit of bandits about to ambush a traveller laden with rich merchandise.

And then we thought of Dorsetshire, that county in which so many names of places are poems. We had only been through it in the train. We had never walked it. We had read Thomas Hardy, but could not take quite such a gloomy view of his own county as he did himself. Surely in this county of lovely names there must be something besides adultery, suicide, and assassination as side-lines to the farming industry. Besides, Dorsetshire is not such a tourists' county as the ones farther west. So we decided on Dorset.

Thus one bright October evening saw us leave the train at Dorchester, close by where Thomas Hardy was then living We stayed the night and walked next day the fifteen miles into Bridport, over the heath, which seems endless when you are on foot. We had no plans, but we realised that if we walked on, clinging to the coast, we should soon be in Devon, whereas we were sworn to 'discover' Dorsetshire. So we looked at a map and turned north towards the little villages with lovely names. And we zig-zagged about, choosing our route each morning, turning now east, now south again, and now north-east.

I think it was on the fifth evening of our tour that the thing happened which has set me writing. We had been taking it easy because I had a sore heel, and we were making for a small town called Ludding Hillow. At night we preferred staying in towns to villages, for in towns there are generally hotels—mostly unlicensed—which cater for commercial travellers of the poorer sort. In these you see the commercial traveller in his carpet slippers eating fried plaice. He knows what he wants and he gets it, and he sees to it that he pays the least possible. These places were therefore much more comfortable and cheaper than the average village inn, where no flight of fancy in the matter of food rises above eggs and bacon, and where they need no lessons in how to charge for board and bed. If we had not to look at every penny we spent we certainly had to look at every shilling.

Well, Ludding Hillow was not for us that night. After the early dusk had fallen we were five miles short of our destination and had reached the village of Changton Margery. What a name! Who christened it and turned a double row of lime-washed cottages into a song? To me the name smelt of wallflowers. I was young and romantic. Perhaps the Golden Girl predestined for me dwelt here. Could anybody resist a girl who came from a place with a name like Changton Margery?

However, it was not romance, but some unromantic blisters, which made me suggest to Bernard that we should stay there the night if we could find reasonable and comfortable quarters. He agreed out of pity for my blisters.

There was one inn of fair size, and it was called The Rose in June.

We entered a large tap-room where half the village seemed to be playing darts and the other half were engaged in shove-ha'penny, and ordered pints of beer. While we were being served we tactfully asked the landlord how much it would cost for supper, bed, and breakfast, because we might possibly want to stay the night in the village instead of pushing on. The landlord said 10s. a head.

This may not seem a lot to those who stay at good hotels, pay half a guinea for their dinner, a guinea for their room, and 4s. 6d. for their breakfast. But believe me, it was a lot for impoverished youngsters like ourselves. Bernard gave me a glance out of the comer of an eye.

'Well, we'll tell you later,' he said, turning to the landlord. 'It just depends on whether we feel like pushing on or not.'

When the landlord had moved away to serve other customers Bernard turned to me and asked how was my heel.

'Pretty rotten, thanks,' I answered, 'I'll sell it to you cheap if you like.'

'No, I was thinking like this. It would be rotten to ask you to crawl into Ludding Hillow tonight. But there might be another place in this village. Do you feel like wandering around and having a look-see? If there isn't we can come back here and throw ourselves on the tender mercies of the proprietor of this palatial establishment. That means bread and cheese and no pickles all tomorrow. But I've a theory that there may be humble citizens who would be glad to cater for our small needs at six bob a head.'

'I'm game,' I agreed. 'I can hobble round the village all right—what there is of it. And at the worst we can always come back here and be stung.'

'Then finish off your swipes and follow me,' sang Bernard; so presently we nodded to the landlord and out we went.

It was pitch dark, and hardly a light showing in any window. Changton Margery was evidently one of those villages where the inhabitants either go to bed or to the local hostelry at sundown—according to funds—to avoid wasting candles. The moon had either gone to bed or had not yet risen. Still, there were stars above and most of the cottage fronts and garden walls were lime-washed, so we could see our way about.

Yet we could not see a likely place where we could stay the night. The small cottages all had that air of containing an agricultural labourer and his wife, two bed-ridden mothers, and a dozen children all crowded into four rooms. The larger cottages—you can always tell by the window curtains and the way the gardens are laid out—looked as if they were occupied by archdeacons' widows who would not only feel insulted but tell the Alsatian about it. It looked to me to be a perfectly hopeless village. There was only the pub.

And then we reached the brow of the hill which marked the boundary of the village street, and on our right was a largish old-fashioned house standing flush with the roadside. A funny, tumbledown old place it seemed, with a high, solid, wooden double gate beside it, arched at the top and spiked, which evidently gave access to a stable yard.

There was a light shining in one of the ground-floor windows, a faint bluish light, which at ordinary times might have given us to wonder what kind of illumination was being used within. But just then we were both thinking of supper and bed, and I was also thinking about my blisters. One cannot be thinking of everything at once.

Bernard went up to the window through which the bluish light filtered wanly on to the road. Then he uttered a view-hallo. Leaning against the top of the lower sill was a card inscribed 'APARTMENTS'. The letters had been cut out of the card so that the light gleamed through.

'Here's what we want,' he said, and strode to the door. He pulled an old-fashioned bell-pull. 'Damn! The thing doesn't work.'

But although he heard no jangle of any bell the summons was answered.

The door was opened slowly, and a woman's voice said, 'Yes?'

I came up and stood beside Bernard and saw that two women filled the space between the door-posts. One was tall and thin and the other was short and stout. They looked to me to be between thirty and forty. Obviously they were sisters. They had the same faces. Had their bodily construction been on the same lines one would not have been able to say which was which. They both had the same squint. And they were dreadful women.

I don't say that because of the squint. 'The most fascinating girl I ever knew used to squint, and no human infirmity ever made me shrink from a fellow creature. But I did shrink back from these. I felt just as if I had found myself in the act of stepping on a snake. Bernard told me afterwards that he felt very much the same about them.

Well, but we were there. We had to make some excuse for calling. Something had to be said, and Bernard said it He told me afterwards that nothing would have induced him to stay there the night. He intended quarrelling about the price of the rooms, however cheap they might be, or finding some fault which would allow us to depart with reasonable dignity. But finding ourselves on the doorstep facing these dreadful sisters we had to pretend to consider the question of taking their rooms.

'Could you put us up for the night?' Bernard asked in a rather queer voice. 'I see you have rooms to let.'

'Yes, we've plenty of rooms, haven't we, Amelia?' said the tall one. 'Come in.'

The short one had burst out laughing, and it wasn't pleasant laughter.

'Plenty of rooms, Lavinia,' agreed the short one, while the tall one laughed just as unpleasantly. We noticed then and afterwards that one sister always laughed while the other spoke, as if at some private joke that we were supposed not to understand.

We entered diffidently. Bernard and I both forget, even if we noticed at the time, how the hall and the rooms were illuminated. We don't remember any lights, but we could see quite well—almost too well, it seems to us now. As we entered and the door closed behind us we were sensible of the atmosphere of the house. It reeked of dust and decay, and of something worse. That dank, earthy smell which one associates with vaults and charnel houses smote the nostrils of us both There was no vestige of furniture in the hall, which was festooned with cobwebs—not so much as a peg on which one could hang his hat, or an umbrella stand. The taller sister threw open a door.

'This is the big sitting-room,' she said, while the shorter one uttered a squeal of laughter.

'Yes,' she echoed, 'this is the big sitting-room,' and the other one echoed her mirthless squeal.

I suppose, really, there was something to laugh about. It depends on the sense of humour. The room was quite bare of furniture or any kind of decorations, and the paper was peeling off walls which were rotten with damp. Neither of us said a word. There seemed nothing to be said. We were shown the smaller sitting-room, which was similar but rather worse. The largest spider I have ever seen ran up the wall like a trapeze artist about to do his turn, as if it wanted to get away from these abominable women. We envied the spider its agility.

They took us upstairs, each taking it in turn to talk to us while the other laughed. The stairs creaked like cheap new boots, and afterwards I found my hand black with the dust off the banisters. The short one threw open the door of another empty room and disturbed a rat, which scuttled over to the fireplace and vanished.

'This is a nice room. It would do well for one of you,' said the tall sister while the shorter one cackled.

'But there's no bed in it,' I protested, 'and no furniture of any kind.'

'I thought young men didn't mind roughing it,' said the short one, while the other laughed.

'Yes, we thought young men liked roughing it,' agreed the other. 'They used to in our day. Many a young man has slept soundly in this room.'

'Yes, and gone on sleeping soundly afterwards,' chuckled the short one.

At which exquisite joke they both exploded in unseemly and mirthless laughter.

'I'm afraid it won't quite do for us,' Bernard said slowly, not knowing what else was possible for him to say.

'There are worse places,' said the tall sister gravely—and this time there was no laughter.

'Yes,' agreed the other in the same sinister tone. 'There is hell, you know.'

I don't know about Bernard, but I suddenly felt extremely sick. In a vague sort of way I wondered how these two creatures lived. The house seemed to be empty of everything except dust and dirt and damp.

'We'd better go,' I said to Bernard.

'Yes, we'd better go,' he answered dully.

'Yes, you'd better go,' agreed the sisters, making the whole thing sound like an incident in one of Maeterlinck's plays, and their abominable laughter broke out in unison.

Downstairs they shepherded us to a side door.

'Do you mind going out this way?' said the taller one, quite quietly and courteously. 'Straight across the yard and out through the big gates.'

I don't remember that it seemed particularly strange to me that they shouldn't be letting us out by the front door. I wanted to go, and I didn't mind how I went. They let us out into the cobbled yard, and fronting us were the high wooden gates which we had seen from the road.

'Good night,' we said shortly and briefly.

'But not goodbye,' squawked the shorter sister.

'No,' squawked the other in the same voice, 'we shall meet again sooner than you think.'

And they both went into paroxysms of sinister laughter, and stood together, watching us go. Mercifully I happened to be looking downwards, and at about the fourth step I sprang backwards and caught Bernard by the arm.

'Hell!' I exclaimed.

Certainly it might have been the entrance to hell if our forefathers' belief in its geographical situation is correct. At our feet, and on our direct line to the gate, yawned an open well. We had been sent to walk straight into it.

We walked round it instead and then turned.

My nerves were shaken up. It was the only time in my life that I have ever sworn at women. I am sure Bernard could say the same for himself. We faced each other—our two selves and the two sisters, they on one side of the well and we on the other—and we called them all the lady-dogs we could lay our tongues to. And the more we cursed them the more they laughed.

Then Bernard said something about calling in the police, and at that word they positively screamed with laughter, as if it were the best joke they had ever heard. And suddenly the strangest possible thing happened.

You have been suddenly cut off on the telephone? Well, the laughter of those two dreadful sisters was cut off in the same way, and the two dreadful sisters weren't there. Where they went we don't know—but we can guess. We found ourselves suddenly and terribly alone in the yard of an empty house. We said nothing—I for one was sweating with terror—and picked our way carefully to the high, double gate.

Out in the road our courage returned. We had some vague idea of knocking up these unpleasant ladies and continuing our remonstrations. But now there was no light in the ground-floor window nor any 'APARTMENTS' card. We tugged at the bell and hammered on the door, but nothing happened. I knew in my bones that the house was empty.

After a little while we found ourselves back at the inn. I don't remember walking there, and I am sure we did not speak on the way. Inside the same crowd was still playing darts and shove-ha'penny.

'Brandy, I think,' said Bernard.

'Yes, brandy,' I agreed.

An ancient labourer was sitting on a chair at the comer of the counter.

'Who lives in that large house up at the top of the village?' I asked him.

'It's an old place with very high stable gates. About two hundred yards from here and on your right.'

'Nobody don't live there,' he replied. 'It's a funny house, that is.'

Privately I couldn't agree with him. I had found nothing funny in it.

'Nobody won't live there neither. They can't let or sell it. Years ago there was two sisters had it, and they used to let apartments to summer visitors. Well, they murdered one poor bloke for his money—smothered him while he was asleep, they did—and then chucked his body down a well. They didn't 'ang for it, as they ought to have done. They was called insane and they died in the asylum.'

'I think another brandy,' I said to Bernard.

'I think so too,' said Bernard.

'And,' resumed the ancient rustic, 'there's a very funny thing about that well. Strangers on 'oliday, just like you might be, are always falling down that well. They've boarded it up and bricked it up, but somebody always comes and takes the boards or the bricks away. Who does it they can't find out. And nobody doesn't seem to know how visitors seem to get into that yard at night.'

'Have a pint,' said Bernard, and added sarcastically, 'Do you know any more funny stories?'

To me he said shortly, 'Brandy again?'

'Yes, thanks,' I said, putting my glass on the counter with a shaking hand. 'Brandy again.'

The Spanish Captain

The old inn had been renamed The Spanish Captain because one had been lodged there in the reign of Elizabeth on his way to London and the Tower. He had come with the first of the four Armadas which Philip flung like gauntlets in the teeth of England. Driven into the bay not three stones' throws from the old house, he had surrendered to fate, bad weather, and the captain of a little English ship of the line which was not much larger than a fishing-boat.

So they named the house after him. What it had been called before that no man can say. But it sheltered the West Country hinds who, remote from wars and even rumours of wars, drank their ale under its roof in peace, and neither knew nor cared what was happening at Towton or Bosworth.

A very fine old house was The Spanish Captain. It wrapped you around with the fragrant atmosphere of old lost things. You entered by going under an arch and turned to either your left or right, according to whether you wanted the coffee-room or the bar. If you went straight on you came out into a long yard with stables—now mostly converted into lock-up garages—on either hand. About a dozen dogs might rush out and bark at you, but they wagged their tails at the same time to show you that they were friendly and only making a noise because they had been brought up to suppose it was their job to do so.

Beyond the yard was an orchard climbing a hill, and if you reached the summit you found yourself at the cliff edge. The apples in that orchard had a 'bite' in their flavour which made you think of the sea on a clear autumn day with the wind blowing in and the spray flying. To the left of the inn was a garden which had once been a bowling-green. It was now littered with broken-down tables and precarious chairs. A notice 'Teas Served' was sufficient explanation.

The Spanish Captain looked proud of itself. It jutted out into the road as if it had taken one pace forward from the level ranks of the shops and houses on either hand. This was inconvenient to motorists, who found it dangerous to drive past at fifty miles an hour. The house, of course, belonged to a brewery, and, while there was a steady flow of trade, both the landlord and the brewers realised that something more could be got out of it.

Private tourists came and raved in refined voices about the old house, but private tourists are apt to do more raving than spending. They have one drink each and possibly a meal. The people who really spend the money are the charabanc parties. They appear out of nowhere, like a shrapnel-burst in a clear sky, spend five pounds in five minutes, and vanish again into the unknown. They don't mind if they drink their beer in a coal-cellar so long as it is beer. There was no pull-in for charabancs outside The Spanish Captain, so most of the parties went down the road to a modem establishment called The Bell, where there was an automatic piano which had to be heard to be believed.

The landlord was a Londoner with a natural instinct for money, and about as much imagination as a cold potato. He dreamed of The Spanish Captain being pulled down and a new one erected in its place with a front thrown back a few yards in order to give the motor-coaches a chance. He communicated his dreams to the brewers and pointed out the business he could do in the summer if his dreams were allowed to materialise.

The brewers also saw the Splendid Vision. They knew that the house was very old and inconvenient. A few tourists stayed there in the summer and a few more made casual calls and had meals, but the brewers were not interested in the sale of meals. So it happened that the youngest director, who was incidentally the son of the oldest director, visited the house to see what could be done, and spent the night there.

Young Mr Panton was a very nice young man, recently married to a very nice young woman. He had been to school at Harrow, but nothing else was known against him. He had a bluff and breezy personality and a very refined voice. Farm labourers and fishermen who had drunk the family beer at his expense were of the opinion that he was a very nice gentleman. Young Mr Panton, driving a modest £700 car and wearing plus-fours and a club tie, arrived at The Spanish Captain on an autumn evening to decide its fate—for its fate was practically in his hands.

Ingram, the landlord, was expecting him, and took him all over the house. Young Mr Panton admired its antiquity but deplored its inconveniences. He quite saw the landlord's point of view. It was all wrong that the summer trade should go to The Bell. Motorists had to go to the inconvenience of parking their cars in the yard. Motor-coaches simply weren't in it. The old place had outlived its time. Knock it down and put up another with space for a good pull-in and all modem conveniences, and you had a house which would wipe The Bell—the property of a rival brewery—right off the map. The local authorities, he knew, would welcome the change.

Young Mr Panton looked around the tap-room. There was an open hearth, beside which seven or eight fishermen and labourers were sitting on two high-backed settles. Young survivors of the Crimea had sat around that hearth and exchanged stories with the veterans of Nelson's fleet and Wellington's army. But the charabanc customers were not going to worry about trifles like that; and you can make a new room look nice and antique by putting in one of those fireplaces of bright red bricks.

'Give these chaps a drink,' said young Mr Panton breezily, and became very popular.

The bay in which the Spanish Captain surrendered is famous for its lobsters. On that part of the coast they knew how to deal with lobsters, for the whole art of cooking and eating lobsters does not consist of drowning them in boiling water and eating them as soon as they are cold. Young Mr Panton had one for his supper, prepared according to local custom, hot, with cheese sauce poured over it. He put whisky on top of this, being just not quite old enough to know better. After a final chat with the landlord he went to bed in a four-poster in a room with a window from which he could have leaned and set swinging the painted sign.

Young Mr Panton was not happy in his bed. He hated four-posters, although, to be sure, there were no curtains The furniture of the house, which had passed on from tenant to tenant at valuation, was not his firm's property. Still he hoped that when the place had been rebuilt Ingram would have the sense to get in some modem stuff. As Ingram probably knew, there was money to be made out of this old junk.

He rolled about on the feather bed and tried to compose his mind for sleep. But he hated feather beds, and it was not long before he became acutely conscious of the hot lobster. Obviously it was a mistake to eat hot lobster and cheese sauce, put whisky on top of it, and then muddle one's head with a lot of thinking about business. He tossed and turned and twisted, with a hundred thoughts quarrelling and pursuing each other through his mind.

The old inn must certainly come down. Business was business. Would Madge remember to give the dog a run? It was a mistake to eat hot lobster at night. Would those shares, which he had bought on information five days ago, continue on the up-grade? Would the Harlequins beat Blackheath on Saturday? What was the story which Lennox had told him in the club last Tuesday? Had he any chance for the Monthly Medal next week?

Curse! It was no use trying to go to sleep. No more lobster suppers!

Might as well light the candle again, smoke a cigarette, and see if there was a book worth reading in the room.

He rolled over, saw that the room was already faintly lit, and that he had a visitor. Strangely he felt no surprise, even when he became aware that the dim light proceeded from the person of this Stranger.

The Stranger was a short man and sallow, with long black hair and moustaches and beard trimmed close to the lips and chin. He wore high sea-boots, and the rest of his costume was neither of today nor of yesterday.

A yellow tunic was buttoned up close against the throat. He made young Mr Panton a deep bow and addressed him in good English with a slight foreign accent.

'Your pardon, senor. My name is Alvarez. I commanded the Santa Teresa. I had on board five hundred soldiers and fifty sailors. Bad weather and worse fortune drove me into the bay out yonder, where I struck my flag to Richard Grenville, a very gallant enemy.

'I was taken ashore and lodged in this house under a guard, ere they took me to London and the Tower, where they showed me the rack and caused me to speak of certain matters of some interest to your country's sovereign. This inn was named after me. It is my only monument. While I was here I was treated with all the courtesy and chivalry due to a gallant foe I beg you, senor, to let the old house stand.'

Young Mr Panton answered nothing, because he found himself bereft of the powers of speech. But he felt nothing of amazement when the Stranger's body partly dissolved and faded, and there was an eddying of mist as if a gust of wind had caught it. And suddenly in his place there stood a very angry lady who pointed a jewelled finger at him and screamed at him alternately in Greek, Latin, and French. Seeing that he was imperfectly acquainted with these languages, she addressed Mr Panton in their common tongue.
This lady was old and hideous and painted. She wore a red wig. Her nose was long and thin and prominent, and her eyes were the eyes of a bird of prey. Her grey gown was sewn all

over with seed-pearls. Her spreading farthingale disclosed ankles covered by the first silk stockings ever worn in England.

'By death and judgment,' she cried, 'I would have thy head for this if I were thy liege mistress today. No, I would but have thee hanged, for thou art one of the common sort. Who art thou to raze a house in which Elizabeth of England once deigned to rest? I am that queen who made England great, setting her as a jewel beyond the reach of thieves, while Philip gnashed his broken teeth at me in vain.

'A poor fool of a squireling met me when I reached the head of yonder street and begged the honour that I should lie in his mean house, which Cromwell's rats ate up five-and-fifty years afterwards. I knew him for a long-eared ass who had not a line of Horace by heart, nor could play a child's tune on the virginals. So I lay there at the inn with my men and women, and there was dancing and singing in the room beneath. Men have forgot the honour I did this house. 'Tis well for thee, Master Jackanapes, that I am already in that land to which thou shalt travel in thy turn, or thou shouldst have cause to remember that I am Harry Tudor's daughter.' She, too, dissolved into a luminous mist, and out of the mist there grew another figure—a male figure—in plain black tunic, trunks and hose, with a narrow ruff about his neck. The hair had receded from his high forehead, and he wore a carefully trimmed moustache and a small pointed beard. He seemed nervous and apologetic. Young Mr Panton thought that he knew the face

'I ask your pardon,' said this new intruder, with a little cough. 'I believe that I am still remembered. I wrote some verses of which I am not ashamed, and a few trifling mummeries for the theatre. I laid here a night. It was a merry evening in the room beneath. I remember that I sang them a song which I had just writ for a clown. It began, "Oh, mistress mine". The face of England is changing past a plain man's belief. I woke tonight because of a whisper which would not let me sleep. They leave so little of the England that I knew and loved. Sir, I am come to you with a plea. I should sleep the easier if the stones of this old house were allowed to stand.'

He bowed and faded, and in his place stood a short, burly, bullet-headed man.

I'm Frank Drake,' he said. 'I did a bit of seafaring and a bit of fighting. I'm not what you'd call sentimental, but I heard the Drum tonight and I knew the enemies of England were at work. The men who knock down an old brick when it needn't be knocked down—they're the enemies of England today. I reached my last port in the bay of Nombre de Dios, and I've slept sound except for a rattle or two on the old Drum now and then. I'm only a rough sailor-man, and you've no call to listen to the like of me, but I'd take it kindly if you spared the house.

'I slept in that bed where you're lying wakeful now. I played bowls on the green outside. Bowls was my best-loved game ashore, although they tell a lie of a match I played on Plymouth Hoe. They've got statues of me about the country, but I don't want statues. My men and me, we'd all sleep the sounder if you men of modem ways would leave something as it was in the country we knew and loved and fought for.'

The next visitant was a lady, a girl of no more than eighteen, and she belonged to a later century than that of the others. Her large round hat was tied on by ribbons which met in a bow beneath her chin. She wore a green riding-cloak over a green gown.

'I am maid and wife,' she said, 'for Richard and I were drowned on the day we had our wedding breakfast here. The cutter which was to take us to Ushant ran into foul weather and sank. I have not found him again in the world I come from. 'Twas a runaway match and my father and brothers were hot upon our heels. We took our last refreshment here while the post-boy who had brought us watched the road for us. There was so much kissing we could scarce take our coffee. It gives me a pleasant pain to linger in the old room below, a shadow unseen by those in the world I have had to leave. I pray you, sir, to pity me and spare the house.'

She gave him one adorable, piteous look and faded into a mist from which emerged the figure of a gentleman clad as if he had stepped out of one of the middle years of the reign of King George the Third—as indeed he had. But his long coat, knee-breeches and belted waistcoat were countrified and ill-cut, and the fourth George would have shuddered at the sight of them. This one wore an empty scabbard at his side.

'I was once squire of this parish,' he said. 'I spent many an evening in the bar with the parson and my near neighbours in the days before the new gentry learned to despise the village inn. I was killed on the bowling-green by Sir Charles Mace. We quarrelled about the points of a setter. He fled to France and presently received his pardon—which pleasured me, for I bore him no ill-will. 'Twas my own fault that I fell upon his iron. Romantic days, some still call them now. But I saw the old inn while the light was fading from my dying eyes. I should be vastly obliged, sir, if you could see your way to let it stand a little longer.'

He bowed gravely, and out of the mist which swallowed him there grew a figure which was singular enough and yet seemed typical of something that Mr Panton had known all his life. It was that of a little bent old man, with matted hair on his cheeks and a ragged white beard. His clothes were nondescript and old enough, but they were not old in the sense of having any historical interest. The figure was an anachronism, but it belonged almost to the present time.

The old man touched the brim of his battered hat.

'Beg pardon, sir, for troublin' you,' he said. 'I'm old Job Mardin. I died two years ago come Michaelmas. They all remembers me round here, and talks of me still, but it won't be for long. I got a nice tombstone in the old churchyard, and my grand-son and grand-darter was going to put up a verse of a hymn, but times bein' bad they found they couldn't afford no more than "Sacred to the memory".

'Most nights, for seventy year and more, I sat in the old tap-room downstairs and drank a pint and played a game o' crib and swapped a yarn or two. They'll all tell you about old Job. I courted my two gals down in the old yard—the one who died and the one I wed. I fought a post-boy over the first 'un, and nigh broke his head against the door of the loose-box where they keeps Trigger today.

'The dead 'aven't got no rights, sir, but they've got fads and sentiments and memories. I've done one or two things which keeps me awake in my grave, but I'd sleep the sounder if I thought the old place wasn't comin' down. You'll excuse me, sir, won't you?'

He, too, faded even as the others had done, and the mist from which he had sprung faded slowly too, like a light frost from a window-pane.

There were no more visitants, so young Mr Panton rolled over restlessly and began to snore.

He wrote to his father on the following morning:

DEAR DAD,
See you the day after tomorrow. I've been all over the house and been into figures with Ingram. I think the house ought to come down. With modern and more convenient premises we could more than treble the summer trade. Give you all details when I see you. Had some hot lobster for supper. Never again! It took me hours to get to sleep, and when I did I did nothing but dream. Don't remember what I dreamed, but I feel like a wet rag this morning.

The rest of the letter does not concern us.

The new inn which now stands in the place of the old one is a building of striking appearance, and the warmth of the red-brick frontage is grateful and comforting to many during the spells of cold weather. There are four doors to it now. One is labelled 'Hotel Entrance', the next 'Saloon', the next 'Jug and Bottle', and the fourth 'Public'.

There is a good pull-in for charabancs in front, and you may see as many as six or seven outside on any fine summer day. Ingram, who now wears his watch-chain farther forward than of yore, is going to send his son to a public school, so that he may become a gentleman, like young Mr Panton.

The interior decorations are splendid, and include the newest of old beams. There is a Maude Goodman reproduction on every wall. And the 'all modem conveniences' are unrivalled in that part of the country.

Oh yes, and they have slightly altered the name of the new premises. The inn is now called Ye Olde Spanishe Captain.

The Bargain

Walton went to the sale because Mrs Walton had seen a carpet, in quite good condition, which would do for one of the spare rooms if it could be had cheap enough. It was one of the early lots, so he arrived in good time, before the auctioneer mounted the rostrum with the air of a judge ascending his throne. Walton said that he always felt that everybody ought to stand up when the auctioneer came in.

With a few minutes to spare he did a little prospecting on his own and noticed a bundle of books. There were about fourteen of them carelessly tied together with string, with the number of the lot—21—stuck on the cover of the uppermost volume. The bundle was rendered more untidy than it would otherwise have been by one book in the middle which was about twice the length and breadth of the largest of the others. There was nothing on the back of the binding to give any indication of its contents.

The books were shabby and not at all interesting on the whole. The Collected Sermons of Dean Widgeon, A Child's Guide to Trigonometry, Half Hours with the Cannibals, by a Missionary, Mother Gruesome's Cookery Book, and so forth. But there was a Wanley's Wonders which Walton coveted.

The book is rare without being valuable. Copies may be had for a few shillings when found, but they are difficult to find. There were no other books on the catalogue and therefore no book-dealers present. He decided to wait a few minutes after the carpet had been put up and see if he could buy *Wanley* at a reasonable price.

The lots were not the effects of any particular person, but consisted of the unwanted 'junk' of a dozen households. Hideous Victorian furniture, still more hideous Victorian engravings, incomplete sets of chinaware, fishing rods, ornaments, clocks, garden implements, they stood in dingy disorder around the room, each waiting for a new home.

The carpet which Walton had been commissioned to buy was Lot No. 8, or, as he preferred to phrase it, 'it went in sixth wicket down.' He was able to buy it at a price at which even Mrs Walton could not complain. About a quarter of an hour later Lot 21 was held aloft by a man in a green baize apron for the bored inspection of the assembly.

Everybody seemed too shy to speak for a few moments, and then a voice tentatively muttered, 'Two shillings.'

'Three,' said Walton crisply.

This advance scared away the opposition. The auctioneer looked around, gave the rostrum a crack with his hammer, and proceeded to become lyrical over the value and beauty of Lot 22—two horsehair armchairs of the 1860 period, one designed for a lady and the other for a gentleman. The bundle of books was Walton's for three shillings.

In due time Walton, the carpet, and the books arrived at the Waltons' house in a taxi. Walton carried the carpet upstairs and left Mrs Walton and one of the maids to play with it.

Then he went down to examine his books.

The *Wanley* was a fifteenth edition, printed at the close of the eighteenth century. Still he had not expected to find a first, and it was the book itself he wanted, not merely its value. All but that and the big flat book he put outside his study door to go down to the kitchen. The maids had a taste in literature which he considered execrable. They liked tales about sheiks who did not suffer from a trouble common to their kind—namely fleas—and who behaved with all the decorum of the nonconformist ministry towards the white girls who fell into their hands; also stories about he-babies who, having been lost in the jungle and reared by apes, grew up to be perfect gentlemen.

Walton reflected that the sermons of Dean Widgeon might do a lot of good below stairs, where the only gleam of religion came by way of the wireless until one of the maids had the presence of mind to turn it off. He liked to think of the cook wrestling with trigonometry—which probably she had hitherto believed to be a difficult and dangerous surgical operation.

Then he sat down and opened the big flat book, and uttered a muffled cry. It was an ordinary scrap-book such as children once used for pasting in the 'scraps' off a Christmas cracker—and probably do so to this day. And the first page he looked at assured Walton that he had a 'find.' He had not collected stamps for many years, and there were few old stamps on which he could have put an approximate value without consulting an up-to-date catalogue, but he had a *flair* which those once addicted to the vice of philately never quite lose.

The turning of every page revealed a fresh discovery. He passed eagerly from page to page and became more and more assured that the contents of the scrap-book were worth many hundreds of pounds, and he soon noticed that no stamp had been issued after 1870.

Obviously the collection had not been made by a boy. Sprightly boyhood would have used gum, mounted the stamps awry, and cut off the corners of some of them to make them look pretty. They were neatly arranged and if they were not all good specimens they were at least clean. The name of each country was written at the head of each page in beautiful old English characters. Walton estimated that the collection numbered some six or seven hundred.

Of course there was a proportion of rubbish; stamps which, despite their antiquity, were still catalogued at from a penny to a shilling, but there were some colonials which would make Redlake's mouth water when he saw them.

Redlake was stamp mad. He had one of the finest collections of British colonials in the country. He had spent tens of thousands of pounds on the contents of the twelve large volumes which he kept locked in a safe. He belonged to the most exclusive stamp clubs; he could smell a forgery as the witch-finder was once supposed to be able to smell out a witch; he could 'sense' the most skilfully mended stamp by touching it with a pair of tweezers. At the mention of stamps he was always liable to start gabbling in the jargon of philately and talk about 'mint' and 'errors' and 'part-worn plate'.

Well, here was something that would interest Redlake. Walton decided that he would show his find to Redlake on the morrow and get the expert to estimate its value.

That night he brought the album into his bedroom for safety's sake. The table beside his bed was already littered with books. Beside the fireplace was another table—a small round one—on which his breakfast tray was placed on those mornings when he was in a lazy mood. His mind was full of stamps when he fell asleep.

He woke—or seemed to wake—suddenly and found himself staring in the direction of the table. With a cold tingle of fear and astonishment he observed that the album was moving, or rather its pages were, as if somebody were slowly turning them. And then that 'somebody' sprang suddenly into the focus of his vision.

It was a very old man who bent gloating over Walton's bargain. He was bald-headed and wore a long white beard. Some kind of dark stuff robe, like a monk's habit, enveloped him from neck to heels. It might have been a dressing-gown. He looked a little like Father Time without his scythe.

But although none of us have any reason for loving Father Time an incarnation of him would not be vile as this visitant was vile. There was something indescribably repulsive about him which dried the saliva in Walton's mouth and set the flesh shrinking back upon his bones. He groped for the hanging switch above his bed and flooded the room with light.

He looked again. The album lay closed upon the table and there was no old man. Mrs Walton, in her twin bed, stirred, moaned plaintively, and slowly woke, demanding to know what was the matter. Walton, in a shaken voice, told her that he had had a bad dream. He always kept brandy in the room and he got out and helped himself to three stiff 'fingers' in a tooth-glass. Then he went back to bed and ventured to turn out the light.

'It must have been a dream ... I suppose,' he assured himself before he fell asleep.

Next morning he took the album round to Redlake. Redlake turned several pages perfunctorily but gave a little start when he came to a page headed 'Ceylon.' He spent five minutes poring over it, and another five minutes over another page headed 'British Guiana.' But it was over the Australasian stamps that he showed most interest. He spent half an hour examining them.

'Well,' he said at last, 'you've got something here! How did you get hold of them?'

Walton explained and Redlake swore, just as Walton had expected.

'Damn it!' Redlake continued, 'some people have all the luck! I've had a few good bargains in my time, but I've never had something for nothing like this.'

'What do you think they're worth?'

'My dear chap, how can I say now? I'm not a walking catalogue, and even if I were, you know as well as I do that you can't trust catalogues. It would take me a month to vet this lot properly. I daresay a lot of them are thinned at the back. As usual the best stamps are bad copies. Look at that Victoria. It would be worth a hundred pounds if some fool of a postmaster nearly ninety years ago hadn't let his scissors run from the margin. Now you'd be lucky to get a tenner for it.'

'Give me a rough estimate.'

'Oh, I daresay the combined catalogue prices would come to about £2,000. Want to sell?'

'We-ell, I don't mind.'

Truth to tell Walton had been out of love with those stamps since the preceding night. He had toyed with the thought of making them the nucleus of a new collection. He had no such intention now.

'I'll give you £200 for them.'

It was a poor offer but not a scandalously bad one. Walton knew that it would take years to sell the stamps piecemeal, and stamps do not bring in interest while they are being kept. Besides, between the buying and the selling thereof there is a great gulf fixed.

'Have a heart!' he urged. 'Make it £300.'

Redlake slowly shook his head.

'I tell you what,' he said presently. 'I haven't had time to examine them, as you can see, but I'll take a chance and offer you £250. Afterwards, if I find I've stumbled on some great rarity, I'll make it right with you.'

Walton considered. He knew that collectors are generally rather less conscientious than race-course thugs, but Redlake was something of an exception. Also Walton had his own reasons for wanting to get rid of the stamps as soon as possible. Another factor was that he had some small but pressing accounts to meet and those grasping gentlemen of the Inland Revenue were keeping up a brisk correspondence with him.

'All right,' he said. 'Done!'

Redlake unlocked a drawer and took out his cheque-book.

Two days later Walton and Redlake met in the street.

'Had another look at those stamps?' Walton asked.

Redlake eyed him coldly.

'No,' he said briefly, 'I've sold them.'

Walton's heart sank. Redlake's superior knowledge, he thought, had earned him a quick dividend.

'Make much on the deal?' he asked casually.

'I lost £70. I took them to Flake and Thorpe's. The dogs saw that I wanted to get rid of them. I suppose they thought I was hard up. Couldn't get 'em to offer more than £180.'

'But my dear fellow, I don't understand. '

'Don't you! Well, come and have a drink and I'll tell you. I spent the whole of yesterday pickling my liver, and I'll have to have another spot now before I can bring myself to talk about it.'

At the back of an adjacent tavern, said once to have been a resort of the poet Swinburne, there was a small discreet room, where young men with golf clubs are generally to be found sitting on the table with swinging stockinged legs. But the room was empty when they entered, and Redlake began the proceedings by lowering a large dark-complexioned whisky as if it were water. Walton noticed that his hand shook.

'Now I can tell you,' Redlake said in a steadier voice. 'I wouldn't have those damned stamps in my house another night even if they were all Post Office Mauritius.

'Before turning in that night I locked 'em in the safe with my collection. Of course you won't believe what I'm going to tell you, but I think you'll give me credit for believing it myself. I'm not the man to lose £70 on a deal in a few hours.

'Well, I went to bed and woke up some time during the night. I couldn't say what time it was. My room's always light unless I draw the blinds, for a street lamp shines right in. I woke up lying on my right side within hand's reach of the table beside the bed. As I became more and more conscious I thought what a queer thing it was that the album I had just bought of you should be there when I distinctly remembered locking it in the safe. Moreover it was open. Then I opened my eyes wider and wished I hadn't. '

A fit of trembling seized Walton.

'There was an old man'

'Yes,' said Walton, 'bald-headed and with a long white beard, something like Father Time—a degraded and repulsive Father Time.'

Redlake jumped like a stranded fish. His eyes bulged.

'How did you know?' he demanded.

'Because I saw him myself. That's why I sold you the stamps, or one of the reasons. '

'Thanks,' said Redlake laconically, 'then I can spare myself the misery of describing the abomination to you. He was sitting on the edge of my bed, if you please, and dabbing his forefinger on a Ceylon stamp in a way no philatelist would touch it. I couldn't see which one it was, but I could see Ceylon written at the top of the page. I'd never believed in things like—like *him* before, and I think I must have felt just as a murderer feels when the procession enters his cell on the morning of his execution.

'This ghastly thing mumbled at me as if he were trying to tell me something, while he went on tapping the stamp. But he didn't make a sound and—he hadn't any teeth. I tumbled out of bed on the other side and rushed into my wife's room where I spent the rest of the night. Next morning I found the album locked up in the safe where I had put it. '

There was a pause.

'Who is he?' Redlake asked in a shaken voice. 'Or, rather, who *was* he?'

'How should I know?' Walton returned.

'I'd like to find out. I'd like to know whether it was he who made the collection or whether that particular Ceylon stamp—whichever it was—is associated with something damnable he once did. I suppose it's impossible to find out now. '

'Over sixty years ago,' Walton commented.

'I know. I dreamed of the old horror three times last night, and I suppose I shall go on dreaming of him for the rest of my life. Walton, I wish he'd had some teeth!'

Walton nodded sympathetically.

'He was the other side of the room when I saw him, and I turned the light on pretty quick. Have another drink?'

'Not here. Let's go back to my place. Did you notice that barman's mouth? Damn people who haven't any teeth!'

A week passed before the two men met again. They encountered in the tube. Redlake looked shaken and ill and his face was a greenish white. He changed his seat and went to sit beside Walton.

'I've just been up to Flake and Thorpe's,' he said.

'Oh?'

'They've just got a New Zealand I wanted. I asked them to try to get it for me three months ago. It's a very fine copy, so they lumped fifty per cent on their catalogue price.'

Walton smiled.

'Well,' he said, 'I suppose it's worth it to you if you wanted it enough.'

'That wasn't what I meant to tell you. Can you stand a shock?'

'What do you mean?'

'They've had some trouble at Flake and Thorpe's. Their night watchman died.'

'Didn't know they'd got a night watchman.'

'My dear fellow, but of course. They've got thousands and thousands of pounds worth of stamps locked up in safes. It was three mornings ago. The manager let himself in and found the poor old chap lying on the floor unconscious. Evidently he'd had some kind of fit, for there was froth on his lips.

'They bundled him to hospital, but he died on the way. Just before the end he became semi-conscious and muttered something about "the old man," and "Ceylon." '

Walton drew a quick, cold breath, and found himself staring straight across the compartment at the comfortable sight of a girl with a well-powdered face, who was reading a book from a circulating library.

'Let's talk about something else,' he said.

House O' Dreams

I was the only day-boy at The Towers at Cornbridge. Old Glendon, the Head, was my father's friend. For my father's sake he broke a rule and took me as a 'day-bug', knowing that the family finances would not admit of my going as a boarder to a first-class preparatory school. So twice a day I went to and fro between our home on the edge of Combridge Common and where The Towers stood within a stone's throw of St Andrew's Church.

There were several ways of reaching the school. The town was roughly rectangular in shape, and The Towers and my home seemed to stand at diagonally opposite comers. There were two short cuts which my father put out of bounds, although I still made frequent use of them. One was through Chippenham Alley, a narrow, winding, ringing passage, in which tramps left their cast-off clothing, with mysterious doors set in the high walls, leading, I now suppose, into the back gardens of houses on either hand.

The other short cut led into the High Street, through a district which was not much better than a slum. I soon found that if I went that way in the morning I met hordes of elementary school children who had no respect for a small boy at The Towers and enjoyed telling him so. But in the afternoon I got out of school a little earlier or a little later than they did, and I found that I could return home by way of Moor Lane and Pentagon Road without the risk of meeting more than one or two stragglers. Very soon I got into the habit of going to school by way of the alley and returning by way of Pentagon Road.

I must describe Pentagon Road It was a double row of dingy, six-roomed cottages, with a tiny general shop here and there, pavements marked out into hop-scotch courts, and a general air of depression and decay. But there was the house which was not small, although it had taken on the air of grimy melancholy of its surroundings.

It stood about half-way up Pentagon Road, and on my left hand as I passed it returning from school. There was a gap in the sad little cottages where a wide frontage of garden stood flush with the edge of the pavement. There was a great iron gate from which I sometimes stopped to pick fragments of green paint which were peeling off. Through the bars one could see the house which stood back behind an untended wilderness of a garden, and it was so smothered with ivy and Virginia creeper that I could only guess if it were built of brick or stone.

The house was by no means a mansion, but it stood back and aloof from its fellows, and towered above them from the height of an extra storey, so that its upper windows were like eyes prying into the dingy back-garden secrets of its humbler neighbours. I had never seen anybody going in or out, but the windows were curtained and no board announced that it was to be let or sold, so I always supposed it to be inhabited. Sometimes I made up stories about it, and half-persuaded myself that it was the secret haunt of coiners or burglars—for in those days my taste in juvenile literature was of a kind which was severely discouraged at home, when I was found indulging it.

At school I was almost unnaturally good. I had had it well drilled into me at home that I was under an obligation to old Glendon for letting me go there, and that the least I could do was to give as little trouble as possible. This I did loyally enough, but having forced myself to be unnaturally good in school, I let off steam outside, and was steeped in all the devilry that a boy of that age could reasonably be expected to find. I was an only child. There was no one at home to play with me, and out of school hours I was allowed to run wild.

I am not boasting of my puerile misdeeds. I must, however, mention one instance of pure devilry and bad manners because of the extraordinary little adventure that followed as a direct consequence.

One afternoon in early summer I was returning home from school by way of Moor Lane and Pentagon Road. It had been, and still was, extremely hot. English history had been torture enough before algebra had given the rack another turn. I had suffered it all with that air of meekness which was old Glendon's principal reward for educating me, but once I was outside The Towers and on my way home the old Adam in me demanded satisfaction.

Outside one of the cottages in Moor Lane an old man sat on a Windsor chair with a stick across his knees. I regarded him carefully as I passed and diagnosed him, correctly as it proved, as being too infirm to run after me. I therefore halted at a short distance and began to 'cheek' him. I blush now to tell of this, and my only excuse is that I was so young a child.

I forget what I said, which is perhaps as well. I only know that from my point of view the experiment was an instantaneous and wonderful success. The old man made no effort to rise, but my words evoked a storm of the foulest and most malignant abuse. I already knew all the bad words, but it was pleasant to hear them again in such volume and so skilfully combined. I remember that I stood lifting my cap and bowing to him at each bellow of blasphemous and obscene invective.

How long it would have gone on I cannot say, but there happened that which put a period to my activities as a tormentor. There was a rumbling noise inside the cottage, and two hobnailed, out-at-elbows boys came tumbling out. They were, I should imagine, the old man's grandsons, and they were two or three years older and much bigger than I.

'After him!' cried the old man, and I cannot write down the name he called me by. I followed Lady Macbeth's advice to the guests, and went at once.

Terror is supposed to lend wings to the pursued, but if it failed me in that I certainly believe that I had never run faster. Had I had anything to fear from two boys of the same age at The Towers I should certainly have been scared, but now I suffered from a dread of the Unknown. I had been brought up in an atmosphere of late Victorian snobbery, and taught to regard all the children of the poor as 'roughs'. In similar circumstances I should have expected a handsome drubbing from two 'little gentlemen', but these young 'roughs' might stick at nothing.

I kept my distance ahead of them until I had turned the corner of Pentagon Road, but from then on age and stamina began to tell. I could hear the pursuing footfalls drawing nearer and nearer, and longed for the sight of a policeman. There was none. I was lost unless a miracle intervened.

None did; but who shall say what a hunted fox will do in his extremity? Inspiration came to me almost at the last moment. The nearest of the two boys was hardly a yard behind me when I swerved suddenly, flung myself against the garden gate of the mysterious old house, and burst into the forsaken garden.

I ran a little way up the path, and hearing no more footfalls, turned gaspingly to look behind me. My would-be assailants stood panting and leaning against the gate, plainly baffled. I saw in an instant that they dared not follow where I had gone.

'Sold again!' I shouted, as soon as I had the breath 'Aren't you coming after me?'

'We'll wait for yew to come out,' one made answer.

'You'll have to wait a long time.'

'Were in no 'urry. Yew'll 'ave to come out somewhen.'

This was true, if poorly expressed. I began to see that I was not yet out of the wood. Perhaps they would wait for me indefinitely—all night, even. Perhaps they would pretend to go away and lurk for me behind a comer. Having carefully weighed the pros and cons, I decided that my best course was to walk up to the front door, knock, and seek grown-up intervention by explaining that I had been wantonly pursued by two big boys of the lower orders. This scheme I immediately began to put into operation.

A voice from the gate reached me as I set foot on the steps.

" 'Ere, boy, don't you go an' knock there. The ghost'll get yew!'

I knew better than to be taken in by that kind of gammon.

'Rats!' I shouted back.

Then I heard the other boy exclaim:

'Cool 'E's goin' ter!'

I reached for the knocker and rapped smartly. As I did so I was looking half over my shoulder and saw the two boys vanish from the gate in obvious panic. It was no ruse of theirs.

Something in the manner of their departure assured me that they would not come back; indeed, I could hear their hobnails ringing on the pavement and sounding farther and farther away. This, while comforting in one sense, was disconcerting in another. It conveyed a broad hint that some dreadful being inhabited the silent old house. I had half a mind to run, but refrained because of the construction which might be put upon my flight. To the person whom I could already hear approaching the door on the inside it would appear that I had perpetrated the gamin's oldest trick, that of knocking for no purpose and running away. It might lead to my being chased again and this time caught, and I had no mind to rouse the enmity of someone who could strike terror into my late pursuers.

Firm and rather heavy footfalls approached the door, which was opened slowly to disclose the figure of an old woman. I knew her at once by sight, for I had seen her several times about the High Street. I did not then know Mrs Norrocott's name but I had noticed her because of certain queernesses both in her dress and in her manner.

I know little of women's clothes today and I knew nothing then, and it would be impossible for me to say now exactly what was odd in her attire. But there must have been something strikingly unusual for a little boy to have noticed it. There was the same quality of oddness about the indoors dress, or frock, which she now wore, although I don't remember precisely what struck me as unusual. I recollect, though, that when I saw her out she was always muttering to herself and glancing behind her, with her gaze bent rather low down, as if she were looking for a strayed child.

For the rest, she was a broad, squat little old woman with grey hair plastered very flat upon the crown of her head, a wrinkled skin as white as the paper before me, and big dull black eyes which seemed to smile at first as if they knew me, only to harden after a moment.

'Who are you, little boy, and what do you want?' she asked. 'I thought at first it was my son Harry come home from school.'

'Please,' I said, 'two big boys chased me, so I ran in here.'

She regarded me not unkindly, and then her gaze swept the gate at the end of the garden.

'Two big boys, eh?' she said dreamily. 'Well, where are they, then?'

'They ran away when I knocked,' I explained.

'But they may be waiting for you outside, eh?' she asked, with surprising intuition for a grown-up. 'Well, you had better come inside. I have a little boy of about your age, and he will be home from school at any moment now.'

It was heartening to know that she had a son. I cannot say why, but I was afraid to enter that gloomy old house, and still more afraid to refuse. So I crossed the threshold gingerly and entered a dark and dusty hall which lost most of what little light it had when the door closed behind me.

Harry won't be long,' she said again, it will be nice for him to have a companion if you can stay a little while. ' Her manner changed suddenly, and she became at once suspicious and severe. 'What's your name, little boy? Have you got a father and mother? Where do you live and what does your father do?'

She fired the questions at me so quickly that for a moment or two I was confused, but I managed to stammer out the facts that my name was Jack Tyers, that my father wrote books and things, and that we lived near the Common.

'Tyers?' she repeated. 'No, I don't think I know the name. But then I go out so seldom and meet so few people nowadays. I am glad that you seem to be a little gentleman.' Could she but have seen me a few minutes since! 'It will be quite suitable for you to play with Harry. So many vulgar people have come lately to live in Combridge that one has to be careful.'

It would be impossible for me, after all these years, to describe adequately what I saw of the contents of that house, but in imagination I can still savour the musty odours of dust and disusage, rotting floors and crumbling fabrics. I don't mean that the house seemed poverty-stricken, although, as I was soon to discover, Mrs Norrocott kept no servant. It never occurred to me then or later that my hostess was really poor. I think, on trying to look back, that she had let everything go to pieces from sheer inertia.

She took two or three steps across the hall, I following her. Then she stopped, muttered to herself, and looked perplexedly at me as if she were wondering what to do with me for the time being.

'Would you like to go up to Harry's play-room,' she asked, 'and amuse yourself with his toys? He will be home from school very soon now—very soon.'

I considered myself too old for toys in the accepted sense of the word. Nor, if she had stretched the term to cover more manly accoutrements, should I have cared for trying to amuse myself with another boy's possessions. The only fun to be had out of playthings was in owning them. But I acquiesced politely. I could see that she wanted me out of the way, and I was far from comfortable in her presence.

So she picked up a candle from a table and led the way up a staircase with a bend in it, and I was vaguely aware of an old grandfather clock ticking in the comer.

'What school does Harry go to?' I asked her.

'Eh?' She half turned. 'What school? Mr Robinson's.'

I had not heard of it.

'And afterwards he is going to Haileybury—like his father.'

She led me across a dark landing, where I was dimly aware of a clothes-basket lying on its side and of pictures askew, into an incredibly musty room where the blinds were drawn. By the light of the candle I was able to see dingy bookshelves lined with tattered books for children, cupboard doors half open and disclosing boxes piled haphazard within, a great rough deal box standing nearly as high as myself, a rocking-horse, and a great wire fireguard standing before the empty hearth. There was little furniture in the room, and such as there was I could not now describe. But I remember that there were framed and faded oleographs on the walls, pictures calculated to amuse children, but all belonging to a bygone generation. And the dust of ages lay thick over all.

'You will be happy here for a little while, won't you?' said Mrs Norrocott, without a hint of irony in her voice; and with that she left me.

I crossed the room, and for some nameless reason I walked on tiptoe. I examined first the books. They were all very old—bound volumes of boys' journals long forgotten, with engravings of little boys wielding unspliced cricket-bats, The Wide, Wide World, Sandford and Merton, and, of course, Eric. I turned from them to the big box which I found to be full of toys. It was so heavy that I found I could draw myself up and lean right across the edge without overturning it.

Gingerly I pulled out tin engines, mostly broken, tin horses and carts, a windmill and a Noah's Ark, and suddenly found that my small hands were coated with grime. These were all too babyish to interest me, and I wondered what sort of boy this Harry might be. But I found a fort, which was an improvement, and then box after box of leaden soldiers. I began setting them out upon the floor to admire them, for I was not yet quite too old for soldiers.

There were smart guardsmen marching at the slope, green-clad riflemen running at the trail, kilted highlanders with fixed bayonets held at the ready, cavalry with movable arms, some of whom carried lances and others sabres. I suppose I played with them for a while in a sort of way. Then a sense of oppression which I had received on entering that dark and dusty room became too strong for me. I thrust the toys back into the box, all anyhow, I am afraid, and not just as I had taken them out. Then I tiptoed to the stair-head, descended a few stairs, and halted by the old grandfather clock. I had some vague thought of seeking out Mrs Norrocott and asking how long Harry would be, since I was expected home.

I did not get beyond the bend of the stairs, because I was arrested by a noise below me. It was one of the most terrible sounds in the world, but most terrible of all to a child—the sound of a grown person moaning and sobbing. I listened while the cold sweat plastered my hair, and I knew that it was Mrs Norrocott. Presently her voice rose in a quavering whimper:

'Oh, Harry, Harry! Come back to me! Come back to me!'

I could bear it no more, and slunk back again up the stairs, out of earshot of those sounds of indescribable woe. But I did not return to that dark and sinister play-room. I lurked on the landing like a little fugitive, until, at the end of half an hour, I heard Mrs Norrocott's voice calling to me. It sounded quite cheerful and pleasant now, and my faint heart took courage again.

'Are you there, Jack? Will you come down to tea? I don't think we'll wait for Harry.'

So I went down, and her voice directed me to a big dining-room. One end of a long oak table was laid for tea, and I saw that there were three cups and saucers on the tray. I glanced shyly around as I entered and saw that the pictures on the walls—they were oil paintings— all represented soldiers and sailors in blue or red uniforms, and all of them except one seemed to me to be terribly old. This one exception faced me as I sat at table, so that I had plenty of opportunity of studying it.

It represented a man in the red coat of a soldier. He looked quite old to me because of his big moustache, but I now know that he was a youngster in the early twenties. When you are ten all grown-up people are 'old'. I was well enough versed in army uniforms to tell that he was an officer. Those were the days just prior to the Boer War, when red uniforms were the vogue, and we youngsters had never heard of khaki.

'Harry,' said Mrs Norrocott, quite pleasantly from behind the tray, 'is a very naughty boy. I ought to have remembered. He is always being kept in. I hardly ever see him before dusk.'

There was no trace of emotion on her face, so that I almost wondered if my ears had deceived me or if it had been someone else that I had heard crying and moaning. So we settled down to tea—and what a tea it was! If a small schoolboy could have selected his own tea he would have found it there before him on the table, with every want miraculously supplied. Mrs Norrocott, I noticed, ate nothing. But evidently she knew what boys liked.

Presently she caught me looking at the portrait of the soldier.

'That's my Harry,' she remarked, nodding.

I stared.

'But—but he's a man! He's a soldier!'

She laughed quite happily.

'What a funny little boy you are! He's a sailor there. That's a little sailor suit he's wearing. But how funny that you should say that, because he's going to be a soldier when he grows up. ' She paused and smiled at me. 'Like his father,' she added.

I had been taught not flatly to contradict people. There was the portrait of a grown-up soldier and she insisted that it was the portrait of a little boy in a sailor's suit. There was nothing for me to say, but I was attacked by a vague and very unpleasant sense of uneasiness. There was something queer and, to me, unseizable about this old woman and in the atmosphere of the house. I left as soon after tea as common politeness would allow. I could see that, in the absence of Harry, she had no wish to keep me. So she shook hands with me and saw me to the door, and made me promise to come again when Harry was home—a promise which I had no intention to keep. So anxious was I by that time to leave the house that I forgot all about the two boys who might be lying in wait for me.

In those days I was innocent of those things that are commonly called 'the facts of life'. I did not know that it was physically impossible for a woman as old as Mrs Norrocott to be the mother of a boy of my own age. I only knew that I did not want to meet Harry, and that I did not want to enter that uncomfortable house again.

There were two good reasons for my not passing through Pentagon Road when going to, or returning from, school, besides the mere fact that it was out of bounds. The two big boys might still be keeping watch for me, and I did not want to encounter Mrs Norrocott again. In the months that followed I saw her once or twice in the High Street, muttering to herself and looking behind her, but I was successful in keeping out of her way.

One incident which puzzled me occurred towards the end of the summer holidays. Glendon, my headmaster, came to spend the evening at our house, and as a treat I was allowed to sit up for a little while to meet my headmaster on terms of modified discipline. For the most part it was a mere matter of listening while the grown-ups talked, with scraps of conversation flung in my direction now and again to show that my presence was not entirely forgotten. I was a good listener, and presently I heard Glendon say something about 'when old Robinson the schoolmaster lived there'. In spite of myself I broke into the conversation to ask:

'Where is Mr Robinson's school, father?'

My father gave me the half-sarcastic smile which always amused me.

'Nowhere, my boy. He's been dead these twenty years. He was the proprietor of your school ten years before Mr Glendon took it over. '

I opened my mouth, but I knew better than to contradict, although I thought I had good reason to be sure that there was a Mr Robinson who still kept a school in the town. I kept silent and maintained a secret and swelling sense of having 'scored', which I always felt on the rare occasions when I knew that I was right and that the omniscient were wrong.

When I returned to school at Michaelmas I satisfied myself by asking the other boys. Of course they had all heard of 'Robinson's School'. Rotten hole it was, too! Did I know anybody from there? Boys, alas, are like that! It must have been early in November before I encountered Mrs Norrocott again. At least, I don't think Guy Fawkes day was passed, because I had sixpence to spend and meant to lay out my coppers in cheap fireworks. With that intention I started for home by way of the High Street. It was a raw, wet afternoon, already almost dusk, and the lemon-coloured street lamps were reflected in the muddy puddles along the road. The Boer War was then a few days old, and strains of patriotic songs were wafted on the wind, containing threats of what we were going to do to a mysterious personage whose name was pronounced Krewjer.

I could not have gone far. At least I had not bought my little Chinese cannons, squibs, and ha'penny Catherine-wheels when I came face to face with Mrs Norrocott.

She knew me at once.

'Why, Jack,' said she, ceasing to mumble to herself, 'why haven't you been to see us? I am just going home to tea now. Harry will be there, and he wants so much to play with you. I have promised him that you will come.' I shrank from her for no reason that I could have described I tried to make excuses. They were all of no avail. There, in the open High Street, I was this old woman's prisoner.

'Oh, but Harry—think of Harry! Poor boy, he has nobody to play with. Come with me, Jack. You need not stay very long unless you like.' So I went with her because I did not know the way to refuse. I was, in some vague way, ashamed to run from her, and it seemed the only way of escape. Thus, burdened by a sense of dread and by indescribable forebodings I tramped beside her over the wet pavements and through the thin mist of rain which darkened the twilight.

We did not converse. Mrs Norrocott muttered to herself and I said nothing while we traversed a quarter of a mile of High Street and turned north into the slums of Moor Lane and on into Pentagon Road. And something told me that we should enter a dark house, and that Harry would not be there, and that I should be sent up into that ghastly play-room alone. Ghastly is the word I should have chosen had it then belonged to my vocabulary, though exactly why I cannot even now give an adequate explanation. The whole house was redolent of sad, lost things, old beyond the memory of any little boy, and perhaps remembered only by the woman who was bearing me thither to share her company of shadows; but the atmosphere of that room on the first floor, with its toys and its tattered old books was charged with gloom and pathos even more than the portrait haunted dining-room.

We entered the rain-soaked garden, she the captor and I the prisoner, although I opened for her the iron gate and smeared my hands on the wet bars. I could not see a glimmer behind the fanlight, but after Mrs Norrocott's key had rattled in the lock and the door had sprung open before her, I saw a dim, blue speck of gaslight burning behind a glass globe, which sprang to brightness when my hostess stood on tiptoe and turned the tap.

'Harry!' she cried, and raised her voice to cry again: 'Harry!' And 'Harry! Harry!' answered the sad voices of echoes. The old woman turned to me.

'He will not be long,' she said. 'He is always here soon after dusk.

Would you like to go up and play with his toys for a little while? You know the way.'

'Please,' I began, in a shaken voice, I'd rather -'

She cut me short, almost with a snap.

'Oh, nonsense, child—nonsense. Have a nice game—have a nice little game. Harry will be here very soon!'

There was a candle in a silver stick standing on an oak chest in the hall beside a salver full of dusty cards. She lit it and thrust it into my hand.

'You know' the way, Jack,' she said.

My hand that held the candlestick must have been trembling, for as I mounted the stairs the shadows billowed around me like the swirling of dark draperies. The old clock in the comer uttered its slow and unintelligible murmurs of warning and menace as I passed it by. The landing was just as I had seen it before in veiled daylight; I seem to remember that the clothes-basket was still lying on its side. The same cobwebs depending from the ceiling festooned the upper walls; there seemed no more of them and no less. Then I found my hand on the knob of the play-room door.

I should not have entered, but as soon as my footfalls ceased the house was sickeningly quiet, and I guessed that Mrs Norrocott was listening down in the hall below. So I drew a deep breath and crossed the threshold. The room seemed just as I had left it that afternoon in the summer. Its contents and the disposition of its furniture were so photographed on my memory that I could be almost sure that nothing had been moved. The rocking-horse was in its old place to an inch, for I moved it a little and revealed a clean space amid the dust on the floor. Then, with my shadow looming on the wall like a giant, I went over to the great box of playthings and rummaged among the dusty toys. My hand came out clutching a mixed detachment of leaden soldiers, and I knew that they had been left just as I had thrust them back in disorder on the previous occasion, and that no little boy had been there since to play with them.

I was putting them back, struggling with something that wanted to make me cry, when a human voice, glad and gay and heartening to hear, rang out on the floor below.

'Harry, darling; Harry! Oh, what a good boy! Oh, Harry dear, I'm so glad you've come home early.'

It was Mrs Norrocott's voice, and although as she went on exclaiming rapturously I heard no other voice I was conscious of the reaction of relief. It seemed to prove that which I had rather more than doubted—that there was a Harry after all. For just those moments the atmosphere of the house cleared and became normal and friendly.

It seemed to me, now that Harry had come home, permissible that I should go downstairs and meet him. This I proceeded to do, treading the stairs not so heavily as when I had mounted them. While I descended I heard Mrs Norrocott's crooning voice from the dining-room.

'Harry, I've got a nice surprise for you. There's another little boy who's going to have tea with you and play with you afterwards. You'll like that, won't you? Give your old mother a kiss before I call him down.'

The door of the dining-room was open, and it was dark inside. My candle, as I reached the threshold, sent a pale yellow tide of light across the room. Mrs Norrocott stood with her back to me, embracing a tall man in soldier's red. He faced me, towering high above her, his arms about her bent shoulders. He was the soldier in the portrait. Neither seemed to be aware of my presence; at least, Mrs Norrocott gave no sign that she had heard my approach.

'Have you been a good boy at school today, Harry?' she crooned.

And then I knew—oh, I don't exactly know what I knew, except that something was horribly abnormal and wrong. All the bogies which I had half fashioned to frighten myself in the dark took their full shape at last and rose screaming at me. In a dreadful waking nightmare I screamed back at them and dropped the candle and fled. Vaguely I remember a sound like the report of a gun, and it must have been the hall door as I slammed it behind me. I remember nothing more until I reached home, sobbing and breathless and very nearly out of my wits.

I could not tell my father or mother what had happened; I could not then have brought myself to tell anybody. But next day they brought a doctor to see me, and he said I had been over-working. So I was sent to my aunt's at Brighton and had the rest of the term for holiday.

It was at about that time that my father's fortunes improved, so that in January I was sent off to boarding school. During my first term away from home my parents moved to another house in a town nearly a hundred miles distant from Cornbridge. So I never saw Mrs Norrocott again.

Twelve years later, when I was nearly twenty-three, I went to stay in Cornbridge with friends who had lately settled there, and stole a morning to wander by myself around my old haunts.

Very little was changed in Cornbridge and it was good to see and recognise the old names over the shops. Things long submerged floated to the surface of my mind, and at every step I raised the ghost of a dead memory.

I bought cigarettes in a little shop in the market-place where once I had bought sweets and turned out of the High Street into Moor Lane, and so on into Pentagon Road. Half-way up on my left hand stood a furniture van outside the garden of a house which I had good reason to remember. Men in green baize aprons were carrying out pieces of heavy furniture between them, and a young man of about my own age, who looked like an auctioneer's clerk, seemed to be superintending the proceedings. I went up and spoke to him.

'House to let?' I asked. 'I see somebody's moving.'

He eyed me cynically.

'No,' he said, 'somebody's moved; and now they've got rid of the old girl at last I should think they'll pull the old rat-warren down. This junk's going down to the sale-rooms by order of the executors. '

'Whose executors?' I asked.

'Mrs Norrocott's.'

'What, old Mrs Norrocott?' I exclaimed. Somehow I had imagined her to have been dead these many years. 'Has she only just died?'

'Two or three weeks back. Why?'

'Oh, nothing. I used to know her.'

'That's more than I've heard anybody else say. It must have been a long time ago. '

'Twelve years,' I said.

He jerked his thumb towards the open door of the empty house.

'Ever been in there?' he asked. 'While she was alive, I mean.'

'Twice.' I said.

He eyed me with a queer kind of admiration.

'Well, I'll be dashed!' he exclaimed. 'Never met anybody before who could say that. What was she like?'

'Odd,' I said. 'But I expect you know a great deal more about her than I do. Who was she? I never knew that.'

'Oh, she was a real lady, you know,' began my informant, stressing the adjective as if to infer that most ladies were spurious. 'Officer's widow, she was. I've heard she once had a son who went into the Army, too, and was killed in the war in Egypt in 1883. The news turned the poor old thing's brain, and she'd never have it that he was dead. After a bit she forgot that he'd ever grown up and thought he was still a little boy at school. She used to wait for him of evenings to come home—poor old creature! I've heard that when she looked at the portrait of him in his regimentals she could only see a little boy in a sailor's suit. That's how the street kids around here got hold of a story that there was a ghost in the house; and the poor old girl being very queer in her dress and in her ways, they used to shout after her and throw things whenever she went out. That's about all I know. Rare lot of dirt and rubbish there was in that old house. And toys! She'd kept all his old toys.' I lit a cigarette and it took me a long while. I quite forgot to offer him my case. He eyed me queerly as if he had suddenly remarked something odd in my manner—as no doubt there was.

'Would you like to walk over the house?' he asked suddenly. 'I think all the stuffs out now.'

'Thanks,' I said, 'I should.'

We walked together up the long garden and into the empty hall. I turned to a door on my right and peeped into a room where once I had stood with a lighted candle on the threshold. It was broad daylight, but my heart pounded against my ribs, for I could not rid myself of the impression that somewhere close at hand and out of sight an old woman and a little boy, reunited at last, were looking at me.

Then I left my companion in the hall and mounted the stairs to enter the room I knew best of all. It was empty now, and even more dust had gathered, and it seemed much smaller to my mature eyes. I was turning to go when something among the dust on the floor caught my gaze. It was a little toy soldier painted red.

So I picked it up and put it in my pocket, and kept it in memory of a mother's little son who grew up and became a soldier, and was killed.

Passenger on the Eleven-Ten

I can see him quite well in my mind's eye, but I am baffled now that I want to describe him. How does one describe a fellow-creature, entirely commonplace as regards externals, in such a manner as to make others see him with one's own eyes?

Let me do my best—but you will not see him just as I saw him. I guessed him to be past thirty years of age: he was darkish and sallow, and the lack of geniality in his looks did not belie a taciturnity which I was soon to discover for myself. He was respectably dressed in dark clothes almost entirely concealed by an overcoat which was neither new nor yet shabby. His bowler-hat was rather old and the shape struck me as being an antique—but then, I am never sure about bowler-hats.

We were alone together in a third-class compartment. The train was scheduled not to stop between Paddington and Reading. After Reading it stopped everywhere, which, I suppose, made it a convenient train for half-day excursionists—for this was a Wednesday.

I am not a particularly curious person, but I find that my waking mind needs some point of focus. I had carelessly dropped my evening paper and my eye was attracted by a pleasant picture of a pretty Devon cove displayed in the advertisement panel of the carriage.

Thus my gaze passed on to my travelling companion. It was not the first time that I had been so placed, and previously I had beguiled such journeys by trying to guess something about my fellow passengers—their callings, their views on current subjects and suchlike things— and then beginning a conversation, with the object of discovering how far my surmises had been right. So I began covertly to take stock of the man opposite me and to try to deduce as much as possible about him, after the fashion of all the detectives of fiction.

Not a farmer—no. Few farmers in real life have the look of the traditional John Bull, but they have the open-air look about them. A commercial traveller? Again no. Clothes too old-fashioned—and besides, would hardly be travelling at that hour. Scarcely well enough dressed to be a village schoolmaster. They're quite smart nowadays, and besides, they have time to travel only at the week-ends. Certainly not a professional man, such as a doctor or a lawyer, and again, not a man who worked with his hands.

And then I guessed it. The village storekeeper. And he had been up to town partly on business and partly perhaps on pleasure. If so, he seemed to have failed in his pursuit of fun. His waxen face was as dismal as a wet Sunday. Perhaps business was bad with him, or he had private troubles. Oh, but the village shopkeeper he certainly was!

We had almost reached Slough when that conclusion came to me, and it remained to prove it and afterwards, perhaps, to beguile the journey with general talk. I began the game, moving my king's pawn up a couple of squares; or, in other words, I asked him for a match.

He did not answer. Indeed, he gave no sign that he had heard me. And I was about to repeat my application, when something stopped me.

I suddenly discovered that I did not like him.

It is really very hard to define what I mean by that. I am not a prejudiced person by any habit of mind. Nor did I feel that he was a wicked man or one likely to spring a surprise attack on me. In common and simple words, I just did not like being in his company—in the same way, I suppose, that some men cannot bear being in the same room as a cat.

This discovery of my mental attitude towards him gave my mind something else to play with. We were two fellow-creatures who had never seen each other before and would probably never see each other again. Why this revulsion on my part as if he were some sort of reptile—a reptile safe in a cage and unable to spring and strike? I began to wonder if this feeling were reciprocated, and if this was the reason why he had failed to hear my request for a match.

The trouble was that I wanted to smoke, and hardly liked to produce my own matches after having asked for one of his and seemingly met with a tacit refusal. I considered, summoned a little hardihood, shook my coat, and matches in a half-empty box made an audible answer.

'Oh, I've got some, after all,' I muttered, as if I were talking to myself, and took them out.

He gave no sign as I lit a cigarette. He seemed to be looking towards me but not at me. He gave me the impression that if I were not sitting just where I was he would have been looking at the blank wall of the partition behind my head.

'Oh, I don't like you!' I thought, still shielding the match with my cupped hands. 'I don't say you're a bad lot. You don't look it. But I don't like being here with you. You make me creep. Why do you make me creep—you extremely commonplace and apparently quite respectable person?'

If only I had had something to read I should have felt more or less at ease. At least I need not have kept looking at him, and my gaze kept on being drawn to that plain, sallow face. It was embarrassing, although he seemed not to notice. I began to wonder if he would suddenly ask me why I was staring at him—and even that truculent gesture would have been a relief.

He sat almost motionless, although I could not say that he did not move at all. He righted himself after the train rocked him. He eased a muscle here and a muscle there of that complicated machinery which will not have us be quite still for very long, even in sleep. But no more than that. Indeed, I think that if he had made the least gesture of a hand I should have been startled into flinching.

So we travelled for nearly an hour until the train began to slacken its speed outside Reading.

I was going on into Wiltshire to stay with friends, and had only half my journey done as regarded time. After Reading the train would stop at nearly every station. And at Reading I had more than half a mind to get out and change my compartment.

That I did not do so I can put down to a variety of reasons, although I did not know the real one, or the one which weighed most with me. Perhaps he would be getting out there, or at the next stop. Perhaps somebody else would give me—well, comfort, for I know of no other word—by getting in. After all, why should I be driven out by a personality which was quite unreasonably distasteful to me? At the best it would be pandering to a kind of cowardice. And again, if he saw me leave the compartment and enter another he might secretly take offence, and I had no reason for wishing to wound him.

So, still together and alone, we left Reading, and after that I knew there was little chance of anybody else getting in. People get off that train at the country stations, but they rarely get into it.

I am not prepared to say how many stations we had passed since Reading when the thing happened. I am going to give one of the stations a fictitious name and call it Woolbury. As we drew level with the platform my travelling companion began to move. This might have startled me if I had not assured myself that I must see him move sooner or later unless his destination lay beyond mine. The train stopped and he got up, lurched, and went to the door.

I did not for the moment follow him with my eyes, and I do not know whether to regret it or not. I might have had a very disagreeable shock. Looking back, I cannot say if I heard the door open and close. Certainly it was closed when I looked round again, and above the back of his head I saw the station's name in blue upon a dim lamp.

The train halted for a space only of seconds, and it was on the move again before I saw a woman on the platform. I had a fleeting vision of her face, and it had passed before I heard her cry out. I could not guess what emotion dragged that scream from her lips. The window was up, and the wheels just then were gathering momentum. I jumped to the window and wrestled with the strap, but by the time I had the window down and was able to look back there was no more than a receding blur of dull lights behind me.

Well, something had happened on that platform, almost under my gaze; but what? It was food for thought—uncomfortable and possibly unprofitable thought—as the train passed on. I had been strangely impressed by a man who had been my travelling companion for upwards of an hour, and when he had left the train a woman had screamed as if at the sight of him. For all I knew to the contrary I might have been witness to the prelude to a murder.

Time, of course, would satisfy my curiosity as to whether anything very much out of the ordinary had after all occurred. It would be in the newspapers; certainly in the local papers. And having thrown that sop to the questioning child that is in the heart of every man, I reached at last the little station among the downs and heard Templer's voice greet me as I alighted.

I said nothing to him about my journey that night—or, rather, that morning—for I had no intention of keeping him up for more than the duration of one cigarette and one drink. But he saw me looking a little odd and he remarked on it.

' You don't look up to the mark,' he said. 'Feeling tired?'

'Not awfully,' I answered, 'but I've just had rather a queer experience.'

He smiled while I told him, and went on smiling after I had finished telling him.

'Queer things, these antipathies,' he said. 'Dogs get them quite a lot. You've got a canine complex. Go and get psycho-analysed. If you let it grow on you you'll start leaving bones on the floor and biting the dustman.'

'I hadn't antipathy for the man,' I protested. 'I didn't hate him. I'd no reason to. I just wasn't happy in his company.'

'Isn't that just the same thing?' he laughed.

'Yes—and no. I can't explain. And, anyhow, what made that woman cry out when he got out of the train?'

'It was probably his wife. Very likely she noticed that he had left his umbrella behind and was beginning to tell him about it. Wives do.'

It is rather hard to be laughed at when one is mystified and disturbed, but it is better on those occasions to join in with a smile, however unwillingly. I did my best.

'Anyhow,' he said, speaking my own thought, 'if anything happened on the platform there it will be in the papers. At least it will be in our local one if it isn't important enough to be reported in London. It comes out the day after tomorrow, and I'll keep an eye open. Let's see—your train was the eleven-ten out of Paddington, wasn't it?'

'That's right. And Woolbury was the station.'

'Right. Well, we'll see. Wait for the local paper. Of course, there won't be anything in it unless something really serious happened. Even our local paper can't make a story out of a woman letting out a yell on a country' platform. Case of murder or serious bodily harm and we shall hear of it tomorrow night—if not sooner, on the wireless.'

We left it at that, and I woke on the following morning with the disagreeable impression on my mind almost smoothed out by sleep. In the evening there arrived an early edition of a

London paper, but that had nothing to tell me. Clearly no crime had been committed on the platform of Woolbury Station.

But on the following morning Templer, already dressed, came into my room before I was astir, a news-sheet folded behind his back. I knew by the look of him that there was something in it which was pertinent to my experience of two nights since. He saw what was passing through my mind and nodded at me and smiled. It was the queerest smile I had ever seen him wear.

'Something there about Woolbury?' I asked.

'Er—yes,' said Templer quietly; and rather in the manner of a doctor he crossed the room and drew up my blind. 'It will be a shock to you,' he said, turning. 'And—well, if you want to know—it's been one to *me*. I'll tell you first, I think, and then you can read it for yourself afterwards. It's only a paragraph or two, and they're headed "The Faithful Heart"—after the play.

'It's about the death of a woman on Woolbury platform just after your train came in. No, don't get scared. It wasn't murder. There'll be an inquest, of course, but they can only bring in "Death from Natural Causes"—in this case, heart failure, I suppose, it seems that there was an elderly woman named Miss Melliss living at Woolbury, and many years ago she was engaged to the man who kept the little general shop in the village.

'One Wednesday he went up to London to buy the engagement ring, intending to return by the last train. She was at the station to meet him, but he didn't arrive. Next day she heard that he'd been run over and killed. That's all years and years ago. It seems she took it very much to heart and never married, and of late years her mind had become affected. She'd got it into her head that one night he'd be coming home by that last train, and she was always there to meet him.

'The people at the station hadn't the heart to turn her away, and everybody knew her story. It seemed to console her to go and meet that train, and if she were disappointed she never showed it.

'Two nights ago, when the train came in—the train you were on—she was there as usual. And just as the train was leaving the porter on the gate heard her cry out and he ran to find her lying dead on the platform.'

He paused and looked at me narrowly, almost nervously.

'Yes,' I said, i heard her cry out. I told you!'

'Well, now, what about the man you travelled down with—the man you didn't feel happy about? Here it is in the last paragraph. "Albert Smith, the porter on duty, hearing Miss

Melliss cry out, immediately ran to her assistance. According to Smith, *no passenger left the train."*

Top Floor Back

Most women who keep boarding-houses have drifted into that vocation through chance or misfortune. You will find that nine in ten do so because they are widows, or because they never married, and because they have not enough money to live on and are quite incapable of earning their livelihood by any other means.

Mrs Skinton, however, was not one of these. She made the keeping of a boarding-house her profession, and studied all the ways and means and small economies with the ardour of a lawyer or a physician who must needs keep abreast of the times. She was an authority on the cost of living, and knew more about the exact percentage which it had risen since the war than any government expert. She had mapped out in exact figures the percentage of profit that each of her boarders ought to, and must, be made to yield by the day or the week. Her guests, had they but known it, were rationed much more strictly than the men in the Services, and the kitchen staff was held accountable for the last ounce of fat and the last half of a potato. If one boarder happened to exceed his or her mathematically exact share it was done at the expense of one of the others.

She called her house a private hotel, the Denbigh Private Hotel and Boarding Establishment. Why Denbigh, she could not have said, except that it sounded well, and the place had to have a name of sorts.

Her charges were cheap enough, Heaven knew. Before the war they were 'from twenty-five shillings a week.' After the war they rose to 'from two guineas a week.'

Externally, and for the most part internally, the Denbigh was exactly like any other seaside boarding house. It was a big, ugly, flat-fronted stone house which faced the sea; or rather, the sea was visible from one window through a chink in the opposite block of buildings. It bore its name in faded gilt letters right across its facade. And Mrs Skinton's clientele was exactly like the clientele of any other such establishment.

In the summer it consisted largely of male and female clerks and shop assistants, down for a fortnight's holiday, who were not too fastidious as to what they ate, used the house only for sleeping in and eating in, and often left under the delusion that they had had a good time. But by the end of September these were nearly all gone, leaving the Denbigh to its 'regulars', with their eternal knitting and never-ending petty squabbles. In confidential moments Mrs Skinton was apt to remark that the house scarcely paid at all out of the season.

Mrs Skinton was tolerably lucky with servants. She cared nothing for their morals or appearance, but chose uncouth sluttish wenches out of whom could be wrung the maximum amount of work for the minimum amount of pay. And, in addition to these, there was Miss Attaway.

Apart from Mrs Skinton herself, Miss Attaway was the oldest inhabitant of the house, in the sense that she had lived there longest. She was a faded, moon-faced woman of forty, almost lacking in any kind of personality save that which was conferred on her by virtue of very prominent front teeth. She liked singing the 'Indian Love Lyrics', and reading problem novels and stories about strong, silent sheikhs. Most people mistook her for a school teacher.

Miss Attaway paid only fifteen shillings a week, but there were reasons for this, the principal one being that Miss Attaway's private and only source of income worked out at something like one pound and threepence a week. But Miss Attaway helped with the light work—as it was called—and did far more than most of the servants. But it suited her to pay a little, instead of being paid, and have her meals in the dining-room, and go on feeling independent and a lady. So everybody was satisfied. Had Miss Attaway been clever and unscrupulous she need have paid nothing, for she alone shared with Mrs Skinton the knowledge of why the top floor back was kept locked.

One bright August morning, when Mrs Skinton had frowned the last belated breakfaster out of the dining-room, she turned to Miss Attaway with the frown still lining her brow.

'I've made a foolish mistake,' she said. 'I've let the room next to the bath-room twice over, and they're both coming to-day.'

Miss Attaway frowned sympathetically.

'Are they both gentlemen or both ladies?' she asked

'One's a lady and the other's a gentleman.'

All the boarders at Denbigh were either 'ladies' or 'gentlemen', except when they happened to be merely children.

'Then I should take the gentleman. They give less trouble.'

'I want to take them both. It doesn't do any good to turn people away once you've said you can take them. Besides, they can claim damages if they happen to know' enough about the law.'

'Couldn't you get the gentleman a bedroom over the way?'

Mrs Skinton shook her head.

'They want a pound each for their rooms. It's sheer robbery. There wouldn't be any profit at all—at least none to speak of. Allowing thirteen and fourpence a week for his food   '

'Well, what are you going to do?' asked Miss Attaway, who seemed to think that every alternative had been exhausted.

'I thought,' said Mrs Skinton, without looking at her, 'I thought of opening up the top-floor back.'

It was a fine bright morning and the maculate tablecloth in front of Miss Attaway was splashed with sunlight, yet she shivered as if a breath of winter had entered the room.

'Do you think that would be—wise?' she asked.

Mrs Skinton did not pretend to misunderstand.

'It was such a long time ago,' she said. 'And I don't believe such things. I was speaking to a clergyman once, and he told me it was wicked to believe such things.'

'There was Mr Hopkins,' whispered Miss Attaway.

'But that was soon afterwards. Somebody must have told him, although they all said they hadn't. He'd heard about it, and then he imagined what he said he saw. This Mr—er—Mr Wilkins, I think it is—who's coming today can't know anything about it. There's only you to tell him, and I know you won't. Why, I doubt if anybody in the town remembers.'

Yes, it was a long while ago, for Miss Attaway was then only twenty-five and still dreamed of being swept off her feet by one of Miss Ethel M. Dell's engaging and masterful heroes.

John Dolland used to sleep in the top floor back. He was a chemist's assistant in the town, and the only 'gentleman regular' at the Denbigh.

Miss Attaway might have cast him for the part of hero in her life-story, but his affections were known to be engaged elsewhere, and Miss Attaway, being of independent means—as she described herself—and a lineage which had its very roots in the Wholesale, could afford in those days to look higher.

Now the lady who had engaged poor John Dolland's affections was of the kind which is sometimes described as 'expensive.' She required and demanded that money should be spent on her. Thus, John Dolland saved none, and when he was suddenly dismissed he had nothing on which to live while he searched for a new situation. And the lady promptly found somebody else able and willing to provide her with chocolates and seats at the theatre and excursions in private motor-cars.

John Dolland might have weathered both these storms if Mrs Skinton had not failed him. When she found that he had no money, and no immediate prospect of earning any, she promptly gave him notice to vacate his room. She did not doubt his intention to pay her as soon as he could, but it was in the middle of the summer season when rooms were scarce and Honesty of Purpose is always a poor second to Ready Money.

Threatened with being turned out penniless into the streets John Dolland reviewed the situation and did that which made Mrs Skinton regret her treatment of him. He sat up in bed one night and shot himself very untidily through the head with a revolver. And then there was an inquest, and a scandal, and awkward questions asked by the coroner, besides people leaving because they couldn't enjoy their holidays in a house where such a thing had just happened.

Mrs Skinton shut up the room, and did not reopen it for several weeks, by which time the household had almost stopped talking about the affair. She then let it to a Mr Hopkins, the advance agent of a small theatrical company. Mr Hopkins spent one night in that room—or part of one night—and left the house next day, bitterly complaining that he had been the victim of something which he supposed must have been a supernatural manifestation. He alleged that he had seen a haggard young man shoot himself with a revolver and then, as Mr Hopkins somewhat tritely phrased it, vanish into thin air.

That was quite sufficient for Mrs Skinton. A ghost may be an asset to an ancestral castle, but not to a boarding-house which depends for its regular patrons on nervous old ladies.

So Mrs Skinton, a little nervous and awed, yet still hardly believing, caused the room to be kept locked. It was annoying to lose the use of a room, but it would be fatal to her interests to have people imagining things and talking and frightening each other out of the house.

'Well, it's just as you think fit,' said Miss Attaway, still doubtfully.

'It's the only thing to be done,' Mrs Skinton rejoined. 'You'd better get on with your dusting as soon as you're ready, and later on in the morning I'll get you to help Emmy prepare the room.'

Thus, after nearly fifteen years, the top floor back was opened once more.

Mr Ernest Wilkins arrived that same afternoon in raiment described in the catalogue from which it was selected as a gent's plus-four suiting. He was a clerk in a London warehouse, and just that type of young man who would necessarily be called Ern or Ernie by his familiars. He said 'Pleased to meet yer' to both Mrs Skinton and Miss Attaway, and was conducted by the latter to his room, where he made no comment on the smell of desuetude which had not quite been scrubbed out of it.

He stayed indoors for the desolating ceremony known as afternoon tea, partly because it saved spending money outside and partly because he wanted to see if there were any attractive young women staying in the house. But the Denbigh was just then unable to produce anything more desirable than an anaemic young lady with adenoids from the glass-and-china department of a Brixton emporium, and Ernie Wilkins, who was something of an Apollo, presently wandered forth in search of adventure.

As Ernie Wilkins was on the eve of an experience which was to shatter his nerves and cause him to be called a liar, with many embellishments, whenever he could bring himself to speak of it, it may be well to describe how he spent the day between tea-time and bed-time, if only to show that he rubbed shoulders all the while with the merely commonplace, and suffered nothing likely in any way to whet his imagination.

After tea he walked out on to the sea-front and bought some picture postcards depicting stout women bathing and inconceivable cads in straw hats to send to his 'young lady' in Balham. Which done, he wandered leisurably up and down, inspecting without apparent diffidence the charms of the young, female human fauna of the town. After half-a-dozen snubs which varied in severity, he engaged the attention of a lady who told him that her name was Ethel; maiden modesty or discretion or both compelling her to withhold her surname.

After a little light dalliance he asked her to meet him by the bandstand at nine o'clock; because by that time they would both have had their evening meal and it would be too late for him to be compelled to spend money by inviting her to the pictures. Ethel agreed, and they parted, Ernie to go on the pier and see if he could scrape acquaintance with somebody even nicer than Ethel. He failed.

At seven o'clock Emie entered the saloon-bar of a public-house nearly opposite the pier, drank two half-pints of bitter, and got into conversation with three other young men who were making holiday together in the town They made an uncertain arrangement to meet on the following day. Conversation with them passed the time until Ernie Wilkins was due to return to the Denbigh for dinner.

When dinner was over—it was made to last fifty minutes in order that the feasters might fail to notice how little they were getting—it was time for Ernie to hurry to the bandstand and meet Ethel. She was not there. She, too, had been looking for a more attractive companion, and she had been more fortunate than Ernie.

He then went on to the pier again, but finding that all the best-looking girls had already been snaffled and only the forlorn hopes remained unattached, he abandoned the pursuit of Venus, drank two more half-pints of bitter, and finished the second just as the landlord was shouting, 'Time, gentlemen!' in a veritable frenzy of inhospitality.

He then returned to the Denbigh on desultory feet, to be warned by Miss Attaway that the electric light was turned off at the meter at eleven o'clock and that candles were not allowed. It was therefore good policy to retire immediately to bed while light was obtainable for the purpose of undressing.

The unaccustomed sea air helped Emie Wilkins to fall asleep almost immediately, and he slept soundly until he woke with a start some two or three hours later.

He was lying on his back, and discovered that he had wakened to a leaden sense of depression and a vague discomfort which was still horribly palpable.

A bluish light was shining on the ceiling at the far end of the room, bright enough for him to trace the cracks which crossed and criss-crossed the plaster. He stared at it, scarcely thinking for a while, before he found himself wondering idly if the moon had risen. This directed his gaze to the windows on his right hand, and he saw only a dull and leaden gleam diffused by the night skies which had clouded over. Curiosity attacked Ernie Wilkins, and he struggled on to an elbow to see whence the light on the ceiling proceeded. Then he caught his breath with a sudden shock which jarred him to the soles of his feet, even before it had time to transform itself into panic terror.

The light on the ceiling seemed to be generated by the bed opposite his own. He could see it very clearly. Its back was to the opposite wall and the footrail seemed only to be inches apart. Yet there had been no bed in the room other than his own when he retired.

But this was not all. In the other bed reclined a young man, also on an elbow, who stared straight across at him out of dilated eyes set in a face which mouthed and worked horribly.

Ernie Wilkins remained quite still, cold and drenched with his own sweat.

He could not move and, at first, he could not think. He was numb with this nightmare horror. Then his subconscious mind, groping under the layers of fear, sent him the message which steadied his tottering reason. There was a mirror somewhere, it said; perhaps a wardrobe door blown open. He was looking at the reflection of his own bed, and it was his own self in reflection that mouthed and stared back at him.

Gasping with relief, but still tingling with the shock, he tried an experiment. He lifted an arm and hand. The young man opposite did the same. He could have laughed then, ill as he felt, at the way he had been taken in.

Ah, but only for a moment! The Thing in the bed opposite was swift to prove that whatever it might be—figment of his fancy or visitant from some other world—it was, at least, no reflection of himself. From the hand which it raised there protruded the long barrel of an old fashioned revolver, and as the muzzle travelled to its ear it closed its staring eyes.

There was no noise at all—only a flash. And then the bed opposite was gone, and the man with it, and the light.

When Wilkins next remembered anything he was on the stairs, huddling his snatched-up clothes against his chest.

When Ernie Wilkins had left the Denbigh for good, which he did early next morning, having spent the remainder of the night roaming on the beach, Mrs Skinton said to Miss Attaway:

'All that I can say is that it's very disappointing. I'd hoped to be able to let that room again, and now I shall have to keep it shut up if people are always going to imagine things. What made you tell him about it?'

'I didn't,' protested Miss Attaway, in a low voice of awe.

'Well, how did he know? I don't believe in such things. I don't think it's *right* to believe in them. I told him he'd been dreaming, of course, and that's just what it was. I don't think he expected me to charge him anything.'

'Did you?' asked Miss Attaway, surprised even then at the business acumen of her hostess.

'I had to. If I hadn't he'd have thought that I knew that something horrible happened in that room, and he'd have talked his head off about it.'

'What I can't understand,' murmured Miss Attaway, with watering eyes, 'is the bed he saw opposite his own. It's just where the bed used to be before we moved it to—to alter the room as much as possible. '

'Oh, stuff!' exclaimed Mrs Skinton. 'I can't think what made you tell that young man.'

'I didn't!' protested Miss Attaway, once more.

'Oh, I don't believe you,' Mrs Skinton replied dispassionately.

And that was the unsatisfactory way in which the affair was settled. Mrs Skinton still does not believe Miss Attaway, or says she doesn't. Ernie Wilkins' friends certainly do not believe him, and call him a liar, qualified by many picturesque adjectives, whenever he attempts to narrate his unpleasant experience. And Mrs Skinton still continues short of the guinea a week for which she could let the top floor back, if she cared to, throughout the summer months.

The Chalk Pit

It had ceased snowing, and the garden was a place of enchantment—lawns and paths a level, unsullied white, trees bending like old pilgrims beneath their unaccustomed burdens, the sun-dial swathed over and now a grotesque snowman, the whole a wonderful effect of black and white, with the frost here and there catching gleams from the windows of the house. It was a place for fairies to dance in.

Outside the drawing-room windows, on a covered balcony which the snow had not invaded, a man and a girl stood leaning over the railings, watching the scene. The light behind them threw their shadows far across the dazzling snow, and it was the girl's shadow which Hailwin watched, and marked each slight movement with a lover's eyes. The silence, which had seemed pleasant for a time, began to torment him, for he had much to say, and no great command of words. When at last he broke the silence, there was a strange quality of awkwardness in his voice.

'Well, it's been a jolly time,' he said, without looking at her. 'I wish it was true that tomorrow never comes.'

'You must come down again soon,' said the girl. 'You know how we love to have you here, Billy.'

'Do you really?' he asked quickly; and the eagerness of his tone was unmistakable.

The house behind them was the pretty, unpretentious residence of Gunthorpe, the painter. It was the last night of a pleasant little Christmas house-party, before the exodus of four of the six guests, all of whom had been declaring with feeling that they had had 'the time of their lives'. The Gunthorpes, essentially Bohemians, had gathered others of their kind around them, and understood the art of entertaining better than most society hosts. Ordinary conventions were not practised at Hillside House, and for some days the party had frolicked like a pack of children.

Silence came once again like a barrier between Hailwin and Mary Gunthorpe; and as it grew, both realised with different emotions that it was a barrier difficult to scale or break down. Something waited to be said, and Mary, realising what it was, felt nervous in Hailwin's presence for the first time in her life.

They had been thrown together a great deal since Hailwin had come down, a thing that meant nothing in a house where harmless flirtations were considered as much a part of the day's amusements as billiards or bridge. Mary liked Hailwin, and had certainly flirted with him, but without any intention of doing harm. She had imagined that they had both tacitly agreed to play a game. Until then she had never thought for a single instant that Hailwin had misunderstood her. The thought scared her a little, and made her miserable. She was not in love with Hailwin, but much too fond of him to wish to hurt him.

A strong wind was keeping another fall of snow at bay, and up the long, wooded hillside the trees were bending and sighing. They listened half unconsciously to the melancholy noise, upon which sounds of merriment from the house intruded from time to time. Mary affected to shiver, drew the silk shawl tighter about her shoulders, and made a sudden movement towards the French windows.

'Let's go in,' she said briskly.

Hailwin's hand found hers, and closed on it.

'No, no, not yet!' he begged nervously. 'I want to tell you something.'

She caught her breath, and gave his hand a sudden little squeeze.

'Billy,' she whispered, 'don't tell me! I know! Oh, Billy—dear! I didn't mean this to happen!'

He looked down at her with a kind of blank dismay.

'You mean—you knew what I was going to say?' he stammered. 'I love you! Mary, isn't it any good?'

She was silent a long while, with her gaze bent downwards.

'I—I like you as a friend, Billy; you know I do!'

'That's not what I meant, Mary dear,' he answered, half under his breath; and turned, as if to re-enter the house.

This time it was the girl who was anxious to linger. Now that the ice was broken, she had so much to say, and yet felt almost tongue-tied. She wanted to say something to cheer him, and yet groped in vain after words. She was genuinely distressed and angry with herself. In that moment, pity almost begot in her the love that Hailwin sought.

'Billy,' she whispered, 'I didn't mean to hurt you. I feel horrible about it. You're not angry with me, are you, Billy?'

'No,' he answered gruffly. 'What have I to be angry about? I was a fool ever to dream that there was any hope for me, and a worse fool not to understand that you were only playing with me. Still, it's done now. Let's go in.'

They went in together, blinking at the sudden glare of artificial light.

Mary's eyes were moist and her heart was heavy. Something indefinable in Hailwin's manner told her how deeply he was wounded, and she blamed herself even more than her harshest critic could have done.

She knew, too, that Hailwin was not the only man she had hurt. John Dreeve, who lived half way across the downs, had always been a special friend of hers, but he had not been near the house for days, and had sulked obviously at his last visit when he saw her monopolised by Hailwin. Him, too, she had unconsciously encouraged, caring no more for him than she did for the man at her side.

The way of the flirt is not easy, if she have a heart.

In the drawing-room four people were playing bridge, of whom only 'dummy' appeared to notice their presence. He crossed the room and spoke to Mary, while Hailwin strode across and out into the hall. Mary's brother Dick, coming downstairs from the billiard-room, encountered him there.

'Hallo!' he called out. 'The man I was looking for! I'll give you twenty-five in a hundred up, if you and Mary have done with each other for the evening.'

Hailwin shook his head.

'No,' he said abruptly; 'I'm going for a stroll, if you'll excuse me?'

'In all this snow? I say, where on earth?'

'Oh, just round the village. I—I've got something I want to think over—something that's got to be thought out. Sorry to be unsociable.'

As he spoke, he took down a light overcoat and slipped his arms through the sleeves. Dick came nearer and regarded him closely.

'What's up?' he asked. 'You're looking awfully queer!'

'Yes.'

'Anything the matter?'

'Oh, no; nothing. Don't worry, there's a good chap.'

Dick shrugged his shoulders.

'Cherchez la femme,' he muttered under his breath. 'I shall have to talk to my little sister about this.' Aloud, he added: 'Better take a latchkey, then. The servants are in bed already, and I expect we shall be turning in soon. Mind you do go round the village, by the way—not up on the downs. You won't be able to see your hand in front of you up there, and you'll lose yourself for a certainty. Here, catch!'

He tossed Hailwin the latchkey, and the door slammed a moment later.

'Didn't even say good-night,' Dick commented. 'This is all Mary's fault. Poor old Hailwin, I ought to have warned him. I must have a chat with the poor old chap tomorrow.'

But on the morrow Hailwin did not appear at breakfast, and his bed had not been slept in. They found him lying, with a broken neck, at the bottom of a chalk-pit on the downs.

Mary Gunthorpe was ill and in bed until long after the inquest; and the kindly verdict of Accidental Death was no reassurance to her.

She suffered not only a violent grief at the loss of a man almost as dear to her as her brother, but a thousand vain regrets, and, worse, felt a hideous sense of responsibility. She hypnotised herself into the belief that she had almost loved him, and memory dealt with her relentlessly, taking her back through the irrevocable past a thousand times. She remembered when it had been very pleasant to have Billy near her, when the touch of his hand had given her ever so slight a thrill; when the little, indefinable something which he had lacked seemed almost on the point of materialising.

But this was sorrow, not guilt; and guilt, too, was nearly always with her. Guilt stood between her and sleep, and whispered: 'You made him do it! You led him on, and then cast his love back in his face. You drove him mad with misery, so that he threw his life away!'

When Mary, white-faced and silent, was up and about again, she was for ever asking herself the dreadful question which none could answer: 'Was it an accident? Did he throw himself down in an excess of bitterness, or was it an accident, as the coroner's jury believed?'

'She is worrying herself to death,' the doctor said privately to her father; and the others did their best to reassure her. But the same problem was vexing them, and the false notes in their voices were not lost to the quick ears of the girl.

Half a dozen times Dick walked at night over the ground which Hailwin must have covered. The house stood half way up a steep hill leading to the open downs, and the lane that climbed past the house was flanked with high, wooded banks, so that the trees met overhead. Even on a sunny day parts of it were almost dusk, but at the summit the country was more open, and the chalk-pit lay in a spot bare of trees for some yards around.

'It was dark, and the snow made everything look the same, so he mightn't have seen,' was Dick's verdict, given to his father. 'Besides, he had a pipe in his mouth when he went over. There's just a chance he was lighting it, and didn't see where he was going. But we shall never know.'

'I'm afraid!' said Gunthorpe gloomily. 'He knew the pit was there.'

'But I don't suppose he was thinking,' Dick tried to argue.

The instinct which had made Dick retrace Hailwin's footsteps on the fatal evening also appealed to Mary. She had never been up on the downs at night, and felt a strong desire, which was only half morbid, to walk up through the lane to the edge of the pit and decide for herself what chance there was that Hailwin might have tumbled over accidentally in the dark. She had read doubt in Dick's eyes when he had told her that the tiling was probable, almost certain. She must decide for herself if she were ever again to enjoy happiness and peace of mind.

The opportunity arrived when her father, mother, and Dick were dining with the Dreeves, and she was still too unwell to accompany them. John Dreeve had not been to the house since the tragedy, and they had promised to ask him to lunch on the following day, for Mary fancied that he, too, blamed her for what had happened, and meant to have nothing more to do with her.

When the servants, under the impression that she had gone early to bed, were safe below-stairs, she slipped out and into the drive.

There had been another heavy fall of snow that day, and flakes began again to fall softly as she left the house. It had snowed when Hailwin went out on the night of the tragedy, and the fall had continued for some hours, so that in the morning all trace of his footprints had been blotted out. But it was a night different in character, for now a full moon rode high in the one part of the heavens clear of snow-clouds.

Mary imagined with a heavy heart poor Billy Hailwin going the same way on the night of the tragedy. She could imagine him pausing at the iron gates to take one regretful last look back at the house. Then she pictured his drooping head and loitering footsteps as he staggered up the dark hillside to his death on the summit.

The pitch-dark lane was full of weird sounds as masses of snow fell from branch to branch and thudded softly on the road. They counterfeited footfalls and whispering voices, and a hundred other terrors of the dark. Half a dozen times she stopped to listen and strove to pierce the deep gloom with her eyes.

Panic was hovering near her, reaching out ice-cold hands; and as often as she stopped she was on the point of turning back.

Then it seemed that her senses were not at fault, that someone was indeed walking with her through the lane. She fancied, with a wildly beating heart, that she could detect a faint shuffling of footfalls through the snow—faint, indeed, but quite audible . That sound surely was not made by the wind, or by falling snow from the trees! She stopped again, but heard nothing, and went on, groping her way through the blackness.

Dogged as she was, she was now terrified. She could feel the presence of someone as well as hear it. Someone was walking at the same pace as herself, a few yards in advance. As her ears grew used to the mysterious sounds she could even locate the distance.

Then came a sudden rift in the trees and light in the lane. Above her, the moon looked down through a ragged rift in the moving foliage, and in her path lay a great pool of light, which dazzled her where it lay on the smooth snow. Her heart gave a great leap, and seemed to stop when a figure in front of her walked slowly into the light.

It was the figure of a man, bare-headed and carrying no stick. The head was bowed, the gait and carriage of the body listless. She recognised the figure with a little, half-suppressed cry, even before it turned and she saw the face. It was Hailwin.

He turned and looked at her, and seemed much the same as in life, except that a whole world of mystery and knowledge lay in his eyes. He smiled at her very gravely and kindly, and there was power in the smile to charm away fear, for all the panic evaporated from her blood and left her calm.

He regarded her only for a moment, and then turned again, and went on.

'Billy!' she tried to call out, only to find herself tongue-tied.

She followed, knowing that she was meant to follow, knowing that this was no purposeless phantasm; that Hailwin, dressed as he had been on his last walk, had returned to show her how he had come to meet his death. She walked after him, breathing easily, but strangely alert, hearing him moving before her in the gloom.

Once a doubt seized her lest it should be only a vivid dream, but she heard the trees whispering, and once felt a cold flake of snow upon her face. Then, when the lane came to an end and she reached the open heath at the top, the figure was still walking slowly before her.

She saw it now grope in the pockets of its coat, and take out a pipe, tobacco-pouch, and an automatic lighter, and presently, after a short while, the pouch was replaced.

So occupied had her mind become in these proceedings that she forgot the imminence of the chalk-pit, and looked around suddenly, to see a black void in the midst of the snow. The road, which had now become little better than a rough track, skirted its edge.

The click of the automatic lighter fell sharply upon her ears, and she saw the figure of Hailwin with the head bent low, after the manner of a smoker lighting up. Then he seemed to stumble in a rut hidden by the snow, and the lighter apparently went out. The figure left the track for smoother ground to walk on, and stood almost on the brink of the pit.

Then, as Mary stood watching with clenched hands and craning neck, John Dreeve rose up out of the darkness, and came stumbling towards the figure of Hailwin.

Dreeve looked worn and ghastly. His lips moved as he approached the phantom of Hailwin, but, though the latter seemed to answer him, the dreadful silence was unbroken.

The girl, half fainting with horror, saw both the phantom shapes clench their fists, and then that of Hailwin opened its hands and laughed. It turned from Dreeve with a gesture of contempt, and once more it bent its head, and the flame of the automatic lighter flashed out over the bowl of the pipe. Mary leaped forward, with a moaning cry of terror, as the hands of the thing in Dreeve's likeness shot out suddenly, and the figure of Hailwin went reeling backwards. She forgot for the moment that what she saw now had happened more than a fortnight since; that the figures were but phantasms of Hailwin and Dreeve, re-enacting the hideous tragedy. It was all real to her—hideously real. She made as if to clutch at Hailwin with her outstretched hands, and fear burst asunder the bonds that held her speechless:

'Billy! Mind, for God's sake! Billy! O-oh!'

The figure had disappeared over the brink. It had dropped down, down, down into the chalk-pit. But as she leaned over, trembling and crying, she saw where the lighter had fallen from its hand, and lay on a narrow ledge only a few feet below.

'You've killed him!' she cried. 'You've killed him!'

And, as she turned, she saw a look on the face of the murderer's phantom that afterwards haunted her sleep for many a dreadful night. Then the figure slowly dissolved, like wisps of smoke in the wind—a faded phantasm of the living.

She told her story between sobs on the following day. She could cry now more freely than she had ever been able to since Hailwin's death. She read incredulity in the eyes of her parents and Dick, but that mattered little to her. She knew that Hailwin had met his death at the hands of Dreeve, and no argument could shake her belief in what she had seen.

'You say,' Gunthorpe questioned judicially, 'that he had an automatic pipe-lighter in his hand? I did not know that he possessed such a thing.' 'Neither did I,' said Dick.

'It dropped from his hand,' Mary reiterated, 'and fell on a narrow ledge about six feet down.'

'Then how is it that it was never found?'

'It must have been covered up by the snow,' Mary gasped, 'and it hadn't all melted before that fall we had yesterday. You'll find it, I tell you, father, under the snow, if you look. That will prove'

She broke off, and a fit of trembling seized her.

Gunthorpe nodded at his son.

'You had better look,' he said. 'It is only fair to Mary. If you do not find it, she will have to confess that her nerves have Oh, who's that? Come in!'

The door opened and the parlourmaid entered the room.

'Mr Dreeve,' she said; and stood back against the wall.

Mary started at the mention of the name and stood up, white and quivering.

'He mustn't come in here!' Dick whispered hoarsely, i'll tell him'

But Dreeve was already in the room. He had been a very frequent visitor, and the maid was used to ushering him straight into the presence of Dick or Mary. He looked pale and haggard, as the Gunthorpes had noticed on the previous night, and spoke quickly and nervously.

'Hullo!' he said to Dick, whose burly form almost eclipsed the others in the background, I've come to say—about coming to lunch this morning.

Awfully sorry, but'

His voice trailed away into silence as he caught sight of Mary's white face and streaming eyes.

'Mary isn't well,' Dick said hastily. 'If you don't mind, I think we'd better'

'You did it!' the girl cried, pushing past her father and advancing towards Dreeve. Her voice was almost as harsh as a man's. 'You did it!' she repeated.

Dreeve went back a step, and stammered something in a weak voice.

'Mary, for God's sake!' Dick muttered. 'I say, Dreeve, don't mind what she says.'

But Mary's voice drowned his, and rang relentlessly through the room.

'You pushed him! You met on the edge of the pit, and quarrelled—about me, I think. I saw you! And you pushed him while he was lighting his pipe. Like this!'

She flung out the palms of her hands, and stood like some tragic statue.

There was dead silence in the room. Then Dreeve collapsed backwards into a chair, and began to sway to and fro and sob. Mrs Gunthorpe crossed the room, trembling, and led her daughter out. The two men stood and stared at Dreeve in an amazement blent with a kind of pity.

Presently Dreeve began to mutter.

'She knows!' he whimpered. 'Oh, my God, how did she know? There was no one there, only he and I and God, Who saw it all!'

'John!' Gunthorpe cried. 'In heaven's name, what are you saying?'

Dreeve looked up and lowered his hands. His face was grey and soiled with tears.

'She knows,' he said quite simply. 'The truth is out. You'd better send for the police.'

'John!'

'Ah, yes; I know how you feel! I didn't mean to do it! I loved Mary—couldn't you see how I loved her?—and she had no word for me when he was about. I was walking down to the village to post a letter, and I met him all alone on the downs. I could have sworn we were all alone. He stood with his back to the pit, and his heels right on the edge, and ten thousand devils were tempting me!

'I didn't mean to do it. I wanted to feel my fist jar home on his face. But he called me a fool, and told me to play the man. He laughed and half turned away, and started to light his pipe, and his heels were right on the very edge. I thought: "If I push him!" And then ... I shouldn't have known I'd done it, but I felt where my hands had touched him, and I heard a long cry and a soft thud, and'

His voice trailed away into silence, and the two men stood before him quite still and quiet. There was nothing they could say to this young man, whom they had known since his babyhood.

Presently Gunthorpe made an effort, and touched him, not unkindly.

'You must play the man and give yourself up,' he said.

Later in the day Dick Gunthorpe returned from a visit to the chalk-pit. He went straight to his father.

'Well?' said Gunthorpe unsteadily.

Dick opened his hand and showed a metal pipe-lighter, discoloured by exposure.

'It was where Mary said,' he muttered hoarsely. 'None of us knew poor old Billy had one—not even Mary. I found it on a bit of a ledge, inches deep in the snow. She—she must have seen something, father.'

Gunthorpe took the automatic lighter in a hand that trembled.

'We'd better tell her,' he muttered, it will set her mind at rest. She'll know that it was through no direct fault of hers that Hailwin died. I think poor Billy wanted her to know that; that was why he—he must have come back. But we don't know; we get such little glimpses of the after-life. Go and tell her, Dick.'

The Intruder

Brenfield is one of those little Middlesex towns which, finding themselves unable to stave off the encroachments of Greater London, have been slowly surrounded and swallowed by the growing monster. The trams screech along a thoroughfare which was a country road within the memory of the middle-aged. Here and there one still sees rural-looking cottages which somebody seems to have forgotten to demolish.

Denwood House stands halfway down an old road a little remote from modem Brenfield. It is a gloomy-looking house, dingily pretentious after the fashion of the eighteen-fifties, when it was built. Its long, straight front stands at a tangent to a semicircle of drive, which curves from one gate to another and encloses a thick shrubbery of laurels and other evergreens. Tall, unkempt trees rear themselves from the midst of this shrubbery, which, grown with the object of screening the house from the vulgar gaze and succeeding, rendered the interior dark and damp-seeming and depressing. Behind was three- quarters of an acre of garden, again too heavily wooded, and a good lawn, on which genteel ladies in crinolines used to play croquet with mid-Victorian curates.

George Marchand had lived alone in the house for twelve years, with a housekeeper and one maid to attend to his wants, when at thirty-eight he most surprisingly married a girl of twenty, Letty Reynolds, who was perhaps the best lady player in the Brenfield Tennis Club.

Marchand was a partner in a firm of architects in the City. He was a tall, thin, sallow man, quiet in his habits and address, and generally considered rather unsociable. That he and Letty should have attracted one another came as a surprise to everybody. She was a bright happy little mortal, with a host of friends, and an appreciation of 'good times.' Like, however, does not always call to like. She and George were duly married at St Stephen's Church and, after a short honeymoon at Ilfracombe, settled down in the gloomy old house among the furniture which she most certainly would not have chosen for herself.

Letty had her own opinions about the house and furniture, which she only half concealed from her husband. She sighed heavily on hearing that another nine years must elapse before the lease ran out. It was shortly after the war when houses were difficult to obtain and, moreover, there was a slump in architecture. George had done well, and would do well again, but meanwhile it would be hardly right to trouble him about a new house and more congenial furniture.

It was about four days after their return from the honeymoon that Mrs Reynolds came to take tea with her newly-married daughter, bringing with her her cousin, Mrs Ridgelow, the wife of a local doctor. Mrs Reynolds' comments on the furniture, ornaments, and pictures were restrained, but they left no doubt as to what was in her mind.

'I know,' said Letty. 'At one time I should have said I would not be found dead among such things, but poor George isn't too well off" just now. Besides, I doubt if anything would look pretty in these dark old rooms.'

'It's a pity,' said Mrs Reynolds, 'that George had everything ready for you before he met you. Men have no idea how to furnish or decorate a house, but at least you can do a little for yourself. You needn't, for instance, live with those atrocities.'

She pointed to two hideous engravings above the piano, one of which represented four intensely solid looking angels conducting a child to heaven, and the other, its companion, represented one of the angels conducting a similar-looking child over a path beside a precipice.

'I could take them down, certainly,' Letty agreed. 'I don't suppose George would mind. '

'I can't think,' said her mother, 'why he wanted to live in a great house full of furniture. Most bachelors live in rooms or a small flat.'

Mrs Ridgelow looked up in surprise, staring from one to the other in quite evident amazement.

'Why, I thought everybody knew ' she exclaimed. And then she checked herself suddenly.

Letty looked up quickly.

'You thought everybody knew what?'

Mrs Ridgelow looked confused.

'I oughtn't to have spoken,' she said 'I thought you knew. Er—George didn't choose the furniture himself.'

'But his people didn't live here. They've been dead for years.'

Letty's cheeks were faintly flushed. Her mother shifted her feet uncomfortably.

'I hate mysteries,' said Letty. 'Will you kindly tell me what you were going to say?'

'I think,' said Mrs Ridgelow, 'that you ought to ask George.'

'Oh, George will certainly tell me if I ask him, but he won't be back for an hour or two yet. And as everybody seems to know'

Mrs Ridgelow glanced uncomfortably at Letty's mother, but there was no help there.

'I suppose,' said Mrs Reynolds deliberately, 'that this is not the first time George contemplated matrimony. It would be strange if it were. He must be getting on for forty. '

Mrs Ridgelow nodded without looking at Letty.

'It's twelve years ago now,' she said. 'He took the house for her. She chose the furniture and pictures. When the engagement was broken off he was left with the place on his hands, and went on living there.'

Letty swallowed something, and then laughed lightly.

'I didn't know anything about it,' she said. 'George and I haven't yet exchanged reminiscences about our awful pasts. When I was eight I fell in love with a milkman, but I haven't horrified George by telling him about it yet.'

But she was hurt nevertheless. Later, when Mrs Ridgelow wandered away by herself to explore the garden, Mrs Reynolds turned to discover her daughter in tears. She laid a caressing hand on the slim young shoulder nearest her.

'Letty dear,' she said, 'don't be foolish. With a man of eight-and-thirty you couldn't expect to be the first.'

Letty dabbed at her eyes with a morsel of handkerchief.

'It isn't that,' she said, sniffing. 'I don't care if George has been in love a dozen times so long as he loves me now—and I know he does. It's the house! I hate and detest it. There, it's out now! I've felt ever since I came into it that there's somebody here who doesn't like me. I—I think it's Mrs Mills, the housekeeper. She's been here all the time. She knew that—that other one.

'Then sack Mrs Mills,' said the practical Mrs Reynolds.

'I can't. George is used to her and likes her. Besides, you can't sack a person for nothing after all those years of service.'

'You'll feel differently in a day or two,' said Mrs Reynolds. 'One can't help feeling unsettled at first. It's all imagination, Letty dear.'

When George came home at half-past six to be kissed and fussed over, the two engravings were gone. He noticed their absence over his wife's shoulder.

'Hallo!' he exclaimed. 'Where're the pictures?'

Letty looked up at him half guiltily.

'You don't mind, George dear?' she asked.

'Not a bit. I expected you to rearrange the place a bit to suit yourself.'

'It wants a lot of pretty things. It's all so old and stuffy, and sad and gloomy. You never told me how you came to live here, George.'

He saw at once that she knew, and for a moment his gaze wavered.

'Dear,' he said, 'it wasn't that I minded your knowing. It's something I've spent years in trying to forget.'

'Don't tell me then,' she said with swift loyalty.

'I think I'd better I'd rather tell you the whole thing once and for all. I warn you that it isn't very creditable. On the other hand, what is a man to do if he falls out of love? Goodness knows why a man is always considered a cad for backing out of an engagement. The other alternative is to marry the girl and be wretched and make her wretched. '

Letty uttered a little sigh of relief.

'So it was you,' she said, 'who broke it off?'

'I asked to be released,' he said. 'I had to. It wasn't just that I had ceased loving her. I ... I hated her. '

Something like a shiver passed through Letty. She pushed him towards an armchair, and when he was seated in it, bestowed herself on the arm.

'I was only five-and-twenty,' said Marchand, 'when I met her and fell in love with her. A boy of five-and-twenty doesn't always know his own mind. I didn't know mine. I had just recently come into a little money. I had my diploma. The future looked very promising. We were going to be married almost at once. I took the house on a twenty-one years' lease, and bought the furniture. I let her choose it. God forgive me. I made a fool of her!'

Letty looked around her with a queer, strained expression on her young face.

'She chose all these things?' she murmured. 'She sat in these chairs? She helped you to hang the pictures?'

Marchand frowned into the gloom of the old-fashioned room. It was already dusk inside, although the sun had not yet set.

'I never think of that,' he said. 'Well, that's all the story, Letty. I needn't bother you with the ugly details of love declining and of hate growing out of indifference. Goodness knows it was no fault of mine. We can only control our passions. We cannot create them. There came a time when her last word irritated me, when I was nauseated by her endearments. She was untidy, frumpish. She was utterly without taste. I tell you, Letty, through her own sheer stupidity she made me hate her. I went through torments before I nerved myself to get rid of her.'

A sudden sob shook Letty, and she turned tear-dimmed eyes towards her husband.

'George, are you going to say this of me one day?'

He drew her to him and kissed her.

'You darling! Don't you know how utterly different you are? I wish you hadn't made me tell you. You'll always be thinking of her now.'

She shook her head.

'But I shan't be able to help thinking of her sometimes. I wish it wasn't her furniture.'

He kissed her again.

'New furniture's so frightfully dear nowadays,' he said. 'And we shan't be very well off for a few' months. Still, you can buy some pretty curtains, and we might run to a few new pictures if you don't like these.'

'May I really buy a few new things and get rid of some of the old? I shan't feel that the place belongs so entirely to her then. Let's get rid of this basket chair, shall we?'

'Why?'

'Oh, I hate basket chairs. They creak sometimes as if somebody was sitting in them when there's nobody there at all. That one does. You know, George—just one more question. When did she die?'

He stared at her sharply.

'Who told you she was dead?' he demanded.

'Nobody.' Letty seemed surprised at herself. 'But somehow I knew that she was dead.'

'You're quite right,' said Marchand. 'She died three or four months after our engagement was broken off. '

The great blue bowl on an occasional table in the drawing-room was smashed as if by the blow of a mallet. Water was still dripping from the edge of the table when Letty found it. The water-lily, which had floated in it only a few minutes before, was crushed. Fragments of china crunched under Letty's feet as she approached the wreckage.

The drawing-room had been transformed during the past month. Cheap but inoffensive water-colours had taken the place of the gloomy old engravings; the solid ugly Victorian chairs and sofa were covered with bright chintz; but the atmosphere of the room remained sad, gloomy, forbidding. Letty felt it as she stood there in the gaslight, gazing sorrowfully and angrily at what remained of one of her recent purchases. Swallowing her indignation she crossed to the fireplace and pulled the bell.

She was alone that night, Marchand having gone to attend a lodge meeting. He would not be back until nearly midnight, two hours hence. He so seldom left her alone, and she had not the heart to tell him how she hated it. A practical young person, she hated him to think that she was growing fanciful.

It was Mrs Mills, the cook-housekeeper, who tapped at the door in answer to her summons. She was a tall, thin woman of fifty, with an abnormally long neck and a pinched, mottled face. Letty indicated the wreckage to her.

'Do you know how this came to be broken, Mrs Mills?' she asked.

'I don't, madam.'

'You didn't break it yourself?'

'Certainly not, madam.'

'It hasn't been accidentally knocked down,' said Letty. 'It's been deliberately smashed where it stands on the table. I've only been out of the room five minutes. There is not a cat or a dog in the place. How do you account for it?'

The woman grimaced oddly. It was as if she had lost control of some of her facial muscles.

'I don't account for it, madam. And you'll excuse me saying that it's no good your putting it on me or Mary. Neither of us has stirred from the kitchen for the last half-hour. '

The woman was at once scared and truculent. There was defiance in the hard eyes which avoided Letty's gaze.

'She hates me, that woman,' Letty thought. 'She's been here too long. She's jealous of my coming here to take over the management of the house.'

'Very good, Mrs Mills,' she answered quietly. 'Send Mary up to me, please.'

While she was waiting she was conscious of the beating of her own heart. She was angry—and scared. These two women had conspired to spoil the new pretty things she had bought. It was they who had torn the new chintz covers on the chairs—she had been finding a new rent to mend every day—and turned the new pictures askew on their hooks.

And yet—suppose she was wrong? Suppose neither was responsible for the hundred malicious little acts which had taken place in the house during the last two or three weeks. Fear of something vague and unknown, too horrible for her to let it take definite shape in her mind, had been lurking near her for many days and nights, stretching out icy hands to touch her. She had warded it off until now. Queer shadows, the sound of stealthy movements, the sensation of being watched, of just missing something with the sight of her eyes—she had labelled such things as fancies, and put them resolutely away. The dark old house bred and fostered such things. But now nameless fear, battering at the walls of her heart, had almost forced a breach ere Mary entered the room

Mary was a tall, bony woman of thirty-two, with coarse black hair and a pale, unwholesome face. She had been in Marchand's service only a year less than Mrs Mills. She was trembling with some unexpressed emotions, one of which was real or simulated indignation. Mrs Mills followed her into the room.

'I did not send for you, Mrs Mills,' Letty said coldly.

'I know, madam, but Mary was nervous of coming upstairs alone after dark.'

Letty bit her lip to keep it from trembling.

'Nervous of coming upstairs alone?' she repeated. 'What nonsense is this?'

'It's not nonsense, mam,' said Mary, 'I'm scared, and that's a fact. You want to know if I broke that bowl, mam. Well, I didn't, nor did Mrs Mills. And I didn't spill the ink over the carpet last week. That was done in the middle of the night. And I don't pull the pictures down, or hang them lopsided neither. You ought to get up early in the morning, m'm, and see for yourself the state these rooms are in when I come down. '

Letty's hand went involuntarily to her heart.

'But who does these things?' she demanded. 'Are you insinuating that I do them myself?'

'You're just as likely to as me or Mary, madam,' said Mrs Mills. 'Nothing like it happened before you came.'

There was no mistaking the impertinence of the woman's tone. It had a tonic effect upon Letty.

'This is simply unbearable!' she cried. 'Mrs Mills, you and Mary have deliberately conspired to try to annoy and frighten me. Between you you have been making the house intolerable. Also one of you has been in the habit of following me about the house and spying on me, especially after dark or when I am alone. You have been in your master's service a long time, but you have gone too far in showing your resentment at having a mistress. You must both take a month's notice from tonight!'

The two women looked at each other. Then Mrs Mills' pursed lips parted to frame words.

'We won't take notice from you, madam,' she said. 'If the master wants to dismiss us'

'That is another impertinence. He shall dismiss you as soon as he returns home. You may both go!'

Mary turned abruptly in the direction of the door, but Mrs Mills lingered, clasping and unclasping her thin hands.

'You've accused us both falsely, madam,' she said. 'It isn't us that has been annoying you. We were afraid something would happen when you came. There wasn't no trouble in the house before. But now you being here, and her things not good enough for you'

The woman's voice dwindled into silence, and Letty stood facing her stoutly, but trembling in every limb. Another was voicing her own unspoken fear, giving a shape to that which had been shapeless in her mind.

'What do you mean?' she asked, in a queer, strained tone.

'Only what I've said, madam. I've been here years, and been comfortable till lately. So has Mary, but now we both of us will be glad to go. There's someone here who doesn't like you, madam, and it isn't Mary, and it isn't me. We both heard footsteps about the place— footsteps we never thought to hear again. Maybe it wouldn't be so bad if you took the chintz off the chairs and put the old pictures back.'

Letty uttered a little gasp.

'You're both mad!' she said. 'I don't know what you're talking about.'

'Excuse me, madam, but I think you do. I'm naming no names. You don't know who might be listening. But you're a woman yourself. Can't you guess how *she* must hate you?'

Letty summoned all her forces to eject from her mind the invading hordes of monstrous shapes.

'You must both go,' she said. 'I know whom to thank for all this.'

They left her silently. She did not hear the low murmur of their voices until they were half way down the kitchen stairs. Then she rose and opened the door. She could not bear the sensation of being enclosed by the four walls.

Letty heard the two servants go upstairs to bed, saw them pass her open door on their way, heard the landing window close and their footfalls high up in the top storey of the house. Then silence closed about her and she settled herself to endure the eternity of an hour before her husband returned.

She found her place in a book from the library which she had been reading, but her mind, otherwise employed, refused to absorb the strings of words. She read simple sentences over two or three times before their meaning revealed itself to her. Finally she laid the book by.

She was afraid. She was tremblingly aware that her imagination was fighting against her on the side of unknown terrors. She was not without courage. She could have faced a fact: it was a shadowy suspicion which cowed her. The demeanour of the servants was another force ranging itself on the side of fear. Suppose they had been telling the truth? Suppose she had been harsh and unjust to them?

The gas was turned high, buzzing and fluttering inside the globe. She was grateful for the sound at first, as something homely which broke the grim silence of the house. But after a while the sound irritated her nerves, and she rose and silenced it by turning the gas lower.

As she rose she was aware of a presence in the room watching her. The sensation was not new, but use had not robbed it of its poignancy. She stood quite still under the chandelier for a long moment without daring to move. Malignant eyes were piercing the husk of her body, gloating on the naked fear beneath.

She braced herself and returned to her chair, picking up her fallen book. The house was deathly quiet now.

She employed reason to fight for her. She was Letty Marchand—Letty Reynolds that was—and she was good at lawn-tennis, and she lived in the twentieth century in a London suburb. What she was afraid of was that which any reasonable person must laugh at in the daylight. If she were sensible she would go to bed. But as she was nervous—she admitted that to herself—she was better sitting up dressed in a lighted room.

'You're a woman yourself. Can't you guess how *she* must hate you?'

The words of Mrs Mills mocked her. If it were true! And suddenly her strained ears caught the echo of a hollow malevolent laugh, and her startled gaze probed the shadows in a far corner of the room whence the sound seemed to have come.

There was nothing there—nothing which her eyes could see. And although any sound would have struck sharply upon her strained hearing she listened in vain.

She read three more lines in the book. Of course, it was all nerves. All the time she had been haunted by this terror, George had noticed nothing. He had even laughed at her stories of the torn chintz and of pictures turned or pulled askew. The whispering, creeping, staring presence was the figment of her own mind, or he lacked that fine perceptive sense to which she was a martyr.

Something stirred in the dining-room across the hall. The sound was not to be defined, but it was distinct almost to blatancy. She stood up, steadied herself, and summoned all her resolution.

A lamp was burning in the hall, but there was no light in the room beyond. She crossed the hall while her heart beat twenty times to every step, and flung open the door, casting a pale flag of yellowish light across the room.

All was quiet now. It was as if she had disturbed something which had crept into hiding. But in the penumbra beyond the line of light she saw a picture hanging diagonally on its long cord.

Reason surrendered. There the thing was. Neither Mrs Mills nor Mary had entered that room since she herself had been in it. She hurried back to the drawing-room looking neither to left nor right.

She wished now that she had swallowed her pride and asked Mrs Mills to sit up with her. As it was, until her husband returned, she was to be the sport of something full of malignity and spite. Minute by minute she felt more keenly a presence which was neither earthly nor good.

'Why do you hate me?' her heart cried to something which, she was sure, could hear unspoken words. 'I was only a child of nine or ten when you were here. Is it because I've taken your place?'

Suddenly she found herself speaking aloud, heard her own voice ringing with passion.

'I know! You hate me because I hate you! And I do hate you. I hate you because you were first with him. I hate the gloomy house you chose, and the ugly furniture, and the mean little ugly mind behind it all. I hate'

She checked herself as a new fear assailed her. Surely this wasn't Letty! It was as if some of the evil around her had crept into herself. And as she fought to regain some of her normal sweetness of mind relief came suddenly with the sight of somebody descending the stairs. Mrs Mills had either taken pity on her or was herself nervous.

From her chair she could see part of the staircase through the open door, and now a woman was slowly descending it. She could see at first only the lower part of her, the feet, the long tight skirt. But each downward step revealed more, and presently she saw a bare arm and a hand which glided over the balustrade.

Relief changed suddenly to blind horror as the full figure topped by the head and face revealed itself. It was neither Mrs Mills nor Mary. She was staring up into the face of a girl of her own age, a girl with chalk-white cheeks, a low forehead, and eyes that were luminous and yet dead, like a fish's. Letty stood up, swayed, and. unable to remove her gaze from the thing that leered down upon her, shrieked aloud.

Sharp upon her screams came the sound of her husband's key rattling in the lock. It broke the spell which held her motionless. She rushed blindly out into the hall, passing within touch of the figure on the stairs.

Outside she heard her husband's voice.

'That you, Letty, old girl? I came home early because I thought you might be nervous.'

A moment later she was in his arms, sobbing and crying:

'Oh, George, thank God you've come. *She's* here! *She's* here!'

His face was like a mirror as he held her. He was staring at something over her shoulder. She saw his face stiffen and pale, and clung the closer. A sudden ugly passion was in his eyes. And in that moment a flash of truth revealed itself to her.

'Oh, George, don't hate! I've hated, too. It's our hate that makes her strong to hurt us. Try to pity—to love'

She was hanging upon him, limp. Soon he whispered that they were alone, and carried her into the drawing-room.

'I thought,' he murmured, 'you had seemed nervous lately, that something was frightening you. And I remembered that it was eleven years ago to-day that she—she died. That's why I came back early. I must take you away from here, Letty.'

She reached out her arms to him.

'Yes, take me away. The house wants to be drenched with sunlight and laughter. All the old things that keep her here must go. Early next year I think—I'm almost sure—we shall have somebody with us who will always be laughing. But take me away for the present, George, dear, for I mustn't be frightened now.'

Denwood House is a happy house to-day. The trees are down and the light pours in. Every piece of the ugly old furniture is gone. The old atmosphere is gone, too, and if you pass the gate on a fine day you will hear children laughing on the lawn behind the house

The Pace Maker

There were six of us sitting out under the cedar tree at Fairview, on a breathless, moonlit summer night, when it had seemed to all of us a crime to stay within doors. Coffee-cups and glasses littered the cool, dry grass at our feet, and the shadow of the tree, enveloping us all, spread nearly to the gleaming white bulk of the house.

We had been lazily discussing a variety of subjects, picking them up and dropping them again, like spoilt children surrounded by too many toys. We had begun on psychic research, and had finally reached—by what conversational byways I hardly know—a discussion on the various public schools. Doddman, the tall, thin, kindly, iron-grey man, who sat at Mrs Edmond's feet, was a housemaster at Tirrelstone; so it was perhaps he who led us into discussing the types of boys produced by certain of the great schools.

It was Edmond, harking back to his beloved ghosts, whom we had to thank for the story which I am about to re-tell.

'Talking of schools,' he said, 'it is curious that among all the ghost stories going about now, not one of them comes from a public school. Yet every school old enough to have traditions has its legendary ghost. There was a haunted form-room at Hurlborough when I was there, but nobody ever saw anything. School ghosts seem to begin and end as legends. To me it is quite remarkable that, among all the seemingly well-authenticated stories one hears today, there should not be one with a school for its background.'

Doddman, who had evidently been especially addressed, smiled wryly.

'You forget,' he said, 'that we pedagogues are compelled to be a cautious people. Whereas a ghost might be a good advertisement to a country house it would hardly be a fortunate adjunct to a school. Boys, when you get to know them, are as nervous as thoroughbred horses, and fond mammas and papas would hesitate to enter their sons at a school which boasted of psychic disturbances. But I could tell you a story.'

A chorus of five immediately began to clamour, and he held up a hand. He seemed a little distressed, and quite unreasonably surprised, that he should be taken at his word.

'I said "I *could*," ' he repeated.

We argued with him for several minutes, and at length we prevailed. He seemed to regret that he had spoken, but he had not the will to stand out against the five of us.

'This is an experience of my own,' he said, 'but it also concerns Tirrelstone. It happened this year—only a few months ago. Ghost stories are always retold, so I will not attempt to pledge you all to secrecy. All I ask is that you will change my name and the name of the school.'

Wherefore I have called him Doddman, and the school, Tirrelstone. Apart from names, I give the story as nearly in his own words as a sound memory will let me.

The spring term at most schools is thoroughly hated by masters and boys alike. The weather is generally bad; the boys take little interest in hockey, the game we play for the first two months; they have shaken down into the year's work just sufficiently to get slack, with the knowledge that there is yet another term before the year-end examinations; and there is only a short holiday to look forward to at Easter. That is the term in which the boys seem to give most trouble, perhaps for the reasons I have mentioned.

Not that I can grumble. I don't come into contact with the boys very much except during school hours. They call me 'Pigeon' and—respect me tremendously. My two prefects run the House for me with very few hitches, and I leave it nearly all to them. Other and less fortunate housemasters call mine a 'pianola' house, because it runs itself.

The school stands just outside the village and the buildings are all on the northern side of the road. My House is the last one of all as you come up from the village, so that to reach it you must pass the whole block of buildings. It is called West. Beyond, and still on the same side of the road, are the playing fields, with a cinder track just inside the hedge, running the whole length. This track is just ten yards over a quarter of a mile in length, and this knowledge is invaluable to boys in training for the sports who want to time themselves over certain distances.

One Thursday evening, early in March, I was sitting in my study, toasting my slippers at the fire, when there was a tap at the door, and Harratt came in.

Harratt was my head prefect, a really charming boy of nearly nineteen, good at everything he chose to touch, and a wonderful caricaturist. He is going to Cambridge in October, and his father wants to make a lawyer of him, but I don't think anything on earth will keep him out of the illustrated papers.

I always welcomed him and Oldfield, the other prefect, when they cared to drop in for a chat, so I made him take the armchair opposite mine. He was wearing running shoes and had an overcoat thrown over singlet and shorts, and he edged himself up to the fire like a dog. Evidently he had just come in after a run.

I have mentioned that the boys play hockey during the first two months of the term. The last month is dedicated to training for the sports, which occur in the penultimate week. For that reason, those who wish to train for any particular event are allowed out on the track and playing-fields in the hour preceding night prayers.

'May I speak to you about something, sir?' Harratt asked. 'It's about Peplow,' he added, after I had told him to continue. 'He doesn't seem very well, so I told him he could cut prayers and go straight off to bed.'

'Quite right,' I said. 'What's the matter with him?'

'He says "Nothing". But I found him in the day-room looking as white as a sheet.'

I was a little anxious. A house master is held directly responsible for the health of his boys, and the case of one who had died of pneumonia the preceding term was very fresh in my memory. Boys are queer creatures, and some of them will go about half dead rather than confess that they are sick.

'I'd better go up and have a look at him,' I said.

'Oh, I don't think it is anything very much, or otherwise he wouldn't have gone out running.'

'Oh, then he's been out, has he?' said I, relieved. 'Been overdoing it a bit, perhaps.'

'I don't know, sir. He's just told me he won't run in the quarter-mile. '

'What!' I exclaimed. 'Peplow!'

Now Peplow was a small, slim boy of seventeen, who did not nearly look his age; but he was a heaven-sent athlete. He played wing-three, and had his colours. Since the death of Garfield, the boy who had died of pneumonia, who was easily the best quarter-miler we had ever had, the race was considered a gift for Peplow.

'He says he won't run, and seems to mean it,' Harratt grumbled. 'I can't *make* him. He's too high up in the school for that—and, besides, it's not much use making fellows. It will be rotten bad luck if he won't. There would be a flag up for the House for a certainty if he went for that race. If you'd only talk to him, sir -'

'No, you don't, Harratt,' I said, laughing. 'I don't interfere with that side of the House. I leave that to you and Oldfield. I think he's most probably injured himself by overstraining. If not, he'll probably change his mind again.'

'I don't think he will, sir. Haven't you noticed a change in him lately?'

'How lately? He certainly seems rather serious for Peplow, these days.'

'He's been an entirely different chap since Garfield died, sir,' said Harratt, wriggling uncomfortably, and pushing his bare knees out to the blaze.

'Yes,' I said, 'they were friends.'

'And Garfield, if he had been here, would have won the quarter-mile. He would have won about five of the open events. He was a certain *Victor* Ludorum.'

I pricked up my ears, and looked curiously at Harratt, who was carefully avoiding my gaze.

'Now,' I said, 'I wonder what on earth you mean by that, boy?'

'Well, sir,' he blurted out, 'I think Garfield's death preyed a lot on his mind. And I believe he thinks he oughtn't to win the quarter-mile, because he thinks Garfield ought to have won it.'

It was at least possible. Boys are queer little beggars, and it is impossible to guess the inner workings of their minds. But I said: 'Oh, come! Isn't that a little far-fetched?'

'I don't know, sir. About a month ago I heard the dickens of a noise going on in Number Four Dormitory, where Peplow sleeps. I went in to read the riot act, and found half of them out of bed. I caught two, and dealt out slingers. It seems that they'd all been bunging sponges, soap, and things over into Peplow's cubicle. Next day I discovered why, and I was sorry for the slingers. Peplow had been talking in his sleep, and he'd been talking to—Garfield. I hear he's always doing that, and it's a bit scary for the other chaps.'

'Yes,' I agreed, 'I daresay it is. All right, Harratt, you leave it to me.'

'Thank you, sir.'

All the same, I was not sure what I ought to do. Morbid tendencies in a boy are dangerous, and they are difficult to eradicate. A minute later the bell went, summoning Harratt out to prayers, and me to read them. I don't suppose I should have done anything about it that night, but I was hardly back in my study when Wilson looked in. Wilson is a local practitioner, who also attends the school

I told Wilson about young Peplow, and he nodded and looked wise, as doctors invariably do when they are most ignorant. He muttered something about giving the boy additional interests. One can't do that. A boy's school-life is already cut and dried for him, and he suspects and resents any attempt to 'take him out of himself'.

'I tell you what,' I said to Wilson. 'It's just as likely as not that he's knocked his heart up through over-training. He's in bed now. I wish you'd come up and have a look at him.'

Wilson assented at once. He had a bag with him, containing a stethoscope and other paraphernalia, and up we went. The lights were still on when we reached the dormitory, and I went first into Peplow's cubicle. He was awake, and seemed surprised to see me. He looked ill and worried, his face was white and pinched.

'I hear you're not very well, Peplow,' I said. 'Dr Wilson happened to come in, so I've brought him up to see you.'

He seemed still more surprised; almost alarmed.

'There's nothing the matter with me at all, sir,' he said.

'Then why did you get leave to cut prayers?'

'I mean, I'm—I'm only a bit out of sorts, sir.'

'Well, Dr Wilson'll run the rule over you. Come in, doctor!'

Wilson went in, looked at his tongue, felt his pulse, and ran rapidly over his chest and back with the stethoscope. Then he slapped the boy's   shoulder.

'Nothing much the matter with you, young man. You'd better take a long sleep tomorrow—no early morning prep, for him, Doddman—and I'll send you up a tonic. Good-night!'

On the way downstairs he said to me:

'Highly nervous, but fit as a fiddle otherwise. Nothing organically wrong at all.'

For two days after that I watched Peplow pretty closely. He went out of training and he was the picture of listlessness. And on the evening of the second day I found him alone in the House library, reading—of all things—Tennyson's 'In Memoriam'. It was just the pportunity I wanted.

'Hallo, Peplow!' I said. 'Taking your tonic? How do you feel nowadays?'

'Oh, I'm all right, sir!' he answered wearily.

'Well, buck up, then, man!' I said. 'Are you going to let the House down, or are you going to run?'

I saw him flinch.

'I can't run, sir. But I shan't be letting the House down. Oldfield gets the quarter within two seconds of me. '

'Yes, and so does Babister in the East, and Throstle in School House. Never mind. Have it your own way. And now come along to my library and have a cup of coffee.'

I saw that he did not want to, but he could not refuse. I heard him walking very heavily behind me as I led the way along the flagged passage which divides my part of the House from the boys'. But he cheered up a little at the sight of the fire, and I rang for the butler and ordered coffee and cakes.

While he sipped coffee and nibbled at chocolate cake I talked to him about a number of unimportant things. Then I launched my attack suddenly, as is my way with boys.

'Peplow,' I said, 'you're in some kind of trouble. Will you tell me what it is?'

I saw him start as if he had been stung, and a sudden hunted look came into his eyes.

'No, sir,' he said abruptly.

'My boy,' I continued, 'you are old enough to know that masters are not your natural enemies. I am only asking for your own good. I want to be your friend. It doesn't matter what the trouble is. If you have done anything wrong we will consider this room a confessional, and nothing that is said between us shall be repeated outside. Now, don't you think you can tell me?'

He looked for a moment half-stubborn, half-wistful, wholly afraid. I saw him swallow twice, and then, with only just that amount of warning, he burst into tears.

You must remember, in judging the effect this had upon me, that a boy of seventeen is very nearly a man, and even as a very small boy I had never seen Peplow cry before. I had given him some thorough lickings, and he had taken the wages for cutting football from heavy-handed prefects without a murmur. I was shocked to see him suddenly break down like some hysterical schoolgirl. And I knew, at the same time, that he was thoroughly ashamed, and his shame communicated itself to me. I let him cry until he was exhausted before I said:

'Now, Peplow?'

His lips trembled. He swallowed another sob, and said:

'Please, sir, it's Garfield!'

Having wrung that from him, I proceeded to climb on to my high horse. I said:

'Now, listen, Peplow! Everybody was very, very sorry when Garfield died. I know that you and he were great friends, and I know how firm school friendships can be. But it is wrong— wicked of you to let his memory be an obsession. It would not be right even if it were your father or your mother'

'It's not that, sir!' he interjected quickly. 'You don't understand. Oh, you don't understand!'

'What don't I understand?' I asked. 'Tell me, then.'

He bit his lip and shook his head violently.

'I can't tell you! I can't tell you! You'd say I was mad! You'd have me sent to an asylum! And I'm not mad! Oh, I swear I'm not mad!'

The tone of his voice, the sudden frenzy with which he gabbled the words, the sight of his clenched hands and contorted body, were all inexpressibly painful to me. I answered him soothingly:

'Whatever you tell me, Peplow, I promise not to think that you are mad! Now will you tell me?'

'Well, you see, sir'—it all came in a burst. 'You see, sir, *he won't leave me alone!*'

I experienced a sudden, sharp sense of repulsion, of nausea, as if I had been about to tread on some loathsome reptile. Then reason came and expelled from my mind something which was ugly and formless and unthinkable.

'Who won't leave you alone?' I asked quietly.

His lips scarcely moved, but I heard, very faintly, the one word, 'Garfield.'

Still, I would not believe. I thought he meant Oldfield, that his tongue had slipped over the similarity of the names.

'You mean Oldfield, don't you?' I said, measuring my tone. 'What is the trouble about Oldfield?'

'No, I mean Garfield!' he cried out wretchedly, desperately. 'You don't understand! Oh, I knew you wouldn't understand!'

The ugly thing was back again, and I had to face it. Here was something outside my previous experience. I had dealt before with imaginative boys, but here was a case of something like obsession. I had filled and lit a pipe, and I went on smoking quietly, doing my best to conceal my feelings from the boy.

'Now, Peplow,' I said, 'let me just understand this. You mean you find yourself continually thinking of him, don't you?'

He seemed to have gained confidence, for he answered quickly, coherently, and in a calmer tone.

'It isn't only that, sir. He's always with me. Directly it gets dark he comes. He never speaks, never tells me what he wants. He's always in my cubicle at night; I only just miss seeing him.'

'Ah!' I said, with a long breath of relief. 'You never have seen him then?'

To my dismay he nodded vehemently.

'Yes, sir.'

'Peplow!'

'Yes, sir—twice. Both times on the cinder track.'

I dropped my pipe and recovered it again. I had heard that it was wrong to sympathise with people who suffered from delusions, but upon my life I couldn't help it.

'Tell me,' I said gently.

A fit of shuddering seized him, and he crouched lower over the fire.

'This is Saturday,' he said. 'The first time was Wednesday. You know a lot of us go out before bed-time to train. It's quite dark when there's no moon, and it's been cloudy all this week. Well, as I changed on Wednesday evening and went out up the road, I felt *him* with me. I kept on asking him—but not aloud—what he wanted, but he wouldn't answer. I got on to the track, threw off my coat, and started running, and he was with me all the time. And suddenly I saw him. He was about half a pace in front of me, and looking round into my face. It was just as if he was pacing me, only he didn't seem to be running. It was just as if he was blown along by the wind.

There was only just his face; all the rest was like a thin grey cloud. I never ran like it in my life, but I couldn't shake him off. Garfield always was faster than me. He was with me like that all the way up the track. Why is it, sir? What does he want?'

I avoided answering both questions by asking instead:

'And the next time you saw him, Peplow?'

'It was the next night, sir—Thursday. 'The same thing happened. Afterwards I told Harratt I wasn't going to run in the sports. I can't bear it, sir!'

'Ah, yes, I remember. ' I cleared my throat wondering what I was going to say next. 'Now, Peplow, you must try not to be nervous about yourself. Our minds are just as real as our bodies, only doctors do not understand them so easily. Once you can persuade yourself that this is imagination - '

'But it isn't, sir,' he interrupted. 'I'm glad it isn't in a way, because if it were I should be mad, shouldn't I? And if it was imagination Herrick wouldn't have seen it too, would he?'

'What!' I cried, and I must have jumped half out of my chair.

'Yes, sir,' he went on drearily, 'Herrick saw him on Thursday night—only Herrick doesn't know. Herrick and Jackson went out to time me. It needed two, as it was dark. They set their watches exactly the same, and Jackson stayed at this end to start me, and Herrick went to the other end to sit in the hedge and wait. When I came in, Herrick asked who'd been pacing me. He said he could have sworn he'd seen somebody running beside me part of the way. That's what made me throw it up—going in for the sports, I mean.'

I had to pooh-pooh this, although I hope I did it kindly. Whatever my private thoughts, I had to pretend to the boy that I could tolerate no other theory than that he was victimised by his imagination. But while I exhorted him to use his will-power and put unhealthy thoughts away from him, my own thoughts were leading me into a shadowland the very existence of which I had hitherto doubted.

Peplow's story cast a spell over me, and I brooded under it all the evening, and in fitful waking periods throughout the night. You see, young Peplow had always seemed to me to belong essentially to a wholesome, unimaginative type. I had had a pretty wide experience of boys, and I should have said unhesitatingly that he was one of the least likely to turn neurotic. But either he had strangely developed some *malaise* of the mind or—and here was the ghastly and seemingly impossible alternative that had to be faced—the boy was haunted.

Next morning, when I woke in broad sunshine, with a whisper of spring in the breeze that fluttered my window curtains, I was ready to laugh at all my troubled fancies of the dark hours I had, I told myself, been listening to the vapourings of an overstrung mind. But as the day wore on my uneasiness returned. You see, the impression I had received was not lightly to be brushed aside.

By lunch time I had decided to tackle young Herrick, and this was rendered easy by a villainous Latin prose fresh from his young hand, which I found among the theme-books sent up for me to look through over the week-end.

The day was Sunday, and there was no evening prep., so after tea I sent for Herrick. He was a cheerful, indolent boy of nearly sixteen, one of the sort who find it convenient to remain in a lower form without attempting to do a stroke of work. I gave Herrick a twenty-minutes' lecture, not only about this particular Latin prose, but on his conduct of life in general. And when I had got him into such a state that he would cheerfully have given a week's pocket-money to change the subject, I suddenly changed it for him. Allowing him to think that he had my forgiveness, conditional on his promised improvement, I altered my tone and began to talk to him about games.

He accepted the change with alacrity, and became voluble, going at once to the subject of Peplow's defection, which must have been the talk of the House. What a pity it was he'd strained his knee. (That, it seemed, was the polite fiction which Peplow had circulated.) And there were fellows in other houses saying that Peplow had turned it up because there was a row in the House, and he'd got the sulks about something. As if a fellow like Peplow would be such a scab!

I asked what Peplow's best time was for the quarter mile, and Herrick told me, adding that he had timed Peplow himself. I forget the number of seconds, for I take little interest in running; but I murmured that it was very good, and asked if anybody had been pacing him.

'No, not when Jackson and I timed him, sir. But—oh, that's funny, sir! Now you've mentioned it, I—I had a sort of an optical illusion.'

I encouraged him to go on, and he continued:

'Oh, it was nothing! I was waiting for him at the top end in the dark, with my watch out, for Jackson had the starting time at the other end, and we met and compared notes afterwards. It's almost as good as a stop-watch, sir. Well, I heard Peplow coming, and looked down the track, and he seemed to me to be running in a sort of cloud. And then, as he got nearer, I thought it was somebody running with him, and I wondered who could be pacing him. I was quite taken in, dead sure there were two of them. You know how one's eyes get wonky in the dark, sir. Then I had another squint at the watch to see how the seconds were going, and when I looked up again there was Peplow haring along by himself. Nobody had been with him either, because I asked him.'

'You'll have to get your eyes examined, boy,' I said, and he only laughed.

It was quite clear he was satisfied that he had been deluded, and I dared not arouse his suspicions by cross-questioning him. I turned the boy out at that, and smoked a pipe over the fire, wondering at the state of my own mind, and half believing that Peplow had infected me with his mental sickness.

After all, I argued with myself, if Herrick had no doubt that what he had seen was an optical illusion, why should I not, too, be satisfied? But I was not. The haunted look on young Peplow's face, his utter abandonment when he broke down, his vehement words—all had combined to make an impression on my mind which I felt that nothing could erase. Ruefully enough I thought of the old saying, that those in contact with lunatics almost invariably go mad themselves.

Not to bother you too much with my processes of thought I ended by presenting myself at Thirkhill's to share his cold supper.

Thirkhill was a young assistant-master who was in Orders. He had lodgings in a house in the village. He was a shy, retiring soul whom everybody liked and trusted, and whereas I doubted if any of my crusted contemporaries would treat me seriously, I knew I could rely on his sympathy and understanding. He was a believer in what he bluntly called ghosts, although he would have nothing to do with spiritualism as a cult.

He heard me through very patiently, interrupting me now and again to put an occasional question. When I was done he was silent for a long time, occupying himself by vigorously polishing his pince-nez.

'Well,' he said at last, 'do you want me to express an opinion?'

'Of course I do.'

'Then frankly, I haven't one. It looks to me like an ordinary case of diseased imagination in a boy, to which Herrick's illusion has lent colour. But I don't scout the—er—the alternative theory. You knew Garfield pretty well, of course. What sort of boy was he?'

'He was a very ordinary healthy young animal, with his mind centred entirely on games; a very ordinary and very nice boy.'

'What were his people?'

'He was an only son and an orphan. He used to spend the holidays on a round of visits to uncles and cousins, none of whom he seemed to care much about. He often told me that he wished he could stay on down here.'

Thirkhill nodded, and seemed to fall into a reverie.

'I wonder,' he exclaimed at last. Then, staring past me, above my head, he murmured: 'Nobody knows what happens to the soul after it has left the body. As Christians we believe that it reaches some ultimate destination—but when? There is a condition which spiritualists speak of, and which they call earthbound. They are possibly right. After all, there is not much that is spiritual about the ordinary human boy, whose horizon is bounded by cricket and football and athletics. The school seems to have been young Garfield's only home, the games his only interests, the boys his only friends. Why shouldn't his spirit linger here until it had shed its earthliness? And to whom should it reveal itself if not to its best friend?'

'If such things are possible   ' I began.

'Oh, they're possible enough. So young Peplow talks in his sleep, does he? That may be a sign. I should like to see him when he's asleep.'

'He's in a dormitory. It would be rather difficult.'

'Can't you move him?'

'I might. What have you in mind?'

'I should like to see if I am sensitive to any other presence. But we should have to take care that Peplow did not wake.'

When at last I left him and went home I did some more hard thinking, and on the following day I spoke to Peplow, and asked him how he was. He understood me and said that he was much the same.

'Do you know,' I said, 'that you talk in your sleep?'

'Yes, sir.'

'Well, it disturbs the other boys. It has occurred to me that your cubicle may be connected in your mind with—er—what you have been imagining lately. How would you like to have a room to yourself? You can have the room that Mr Short used to have, opposite the bathrooms if you like.'

He accepted my offer without enthusiasm, and I instructed the matron accordingly. Two evenings later, just before bed-time, I invited him into my room for a cup of coffee; and in that coffee was as strong a sleeping draught as I could get Wilson to provide for the purpose.

Thirkhill arrived by appointment shortly after ten and we must have sat smoking and talking for more than an hour, for it was turned half-past eleven when he suggested that we should go upstairs.

And now comes the strangest part of the story, the part which, when I look back upon it, almost makes me discredit the records of my own memory. If it were not for Thirkhill I think I should easily persuade myself that our experience was some fantastic dream, approaching close to the borderlands of nightmare. For the memory is somehow distant and shrouded, as of something I dreamed years ago, instead of an actual happening a few months since. Strangely enough, Thirkhill's impressions are so sharp and vivid that it is painful to him to mention the subject even to me.

We reached Peplow's room and I went in first and turned on the electric light. The boy was in a sound sleep, breathing very deeply and regularly, but there was a troubled expression on his face. His lips were parted and they moved from time to time as if in silent speech. There was a frown on his brow and a haggard droop to the corners of his mouth. It was anything but a peaceful face.

Seeing that he was unlikely to wake, I motioned Thirkhill to come in. He did so, and, having looked into Peplow's face, sat down on a chair by the chest of drawers. I took the only other chair in the room, which was close to the door and within reach of the electric light, which Thirkhill presently signed to me to extinguish.

There was no moon, but the night was windy and clear. The stars could be seen through the flying veils of white cloud. In the pallid light from the open window the white bed was like a patch of moonlight seen on the floor of a dark forest. A grey pallor overhung the room, in which I could see quite clearly the outlines of the simple furniture, and the crouched, almost motionless, figure of Thirkhill.

I began the vigil with a tingling sensation of awe, but this passed in time as other thoughts took possession of me. To tell the truth, my conscience was not easy. I had deliberately administered a soporific to one of my boys in order to make him the subject of a psychic experiment. Whatever my intentions, that was the bald fact, and if that fact became known

I should find my position a difficult one to defend. One of my fears was that the boy would wake and want to know what we were doing there.

It seemed to me that half the night passed while we waited, although, as we discovered afterwards, our vigil could not have lasted much more than an hour. I was more than ready to go, but I was in Thirkhill's hands, and I waited for him to give the signal. At last, and suddenly, Peplow stirred, and I thought he was waking.

I got upon my feet, but Thirkhill turned to me, finger on lips. Then Peplow began to moan in his sleep, to utter broken cries and scraps of incoherent sentences. He kicked and uttered little whining sounds, such as are made by a dreaming dog. He seemed to be wandering in labyrinths of dreariness and fear. Mutterings merged into groans, and groans into sobs. As I listened I felt a weakness steal over me, and my heart beat like the ticking of a little watch. And amidst a nightmare clamouring of terror, which seemed to come from without and within, I heard Thirkhill's voice raised just above a whisper:

'Garfield, are you here?'

There was no answer—only a plunging and moaning from the boy on the bed.

'Garfield,' I heard, 'if you are here, I conjure you in the name -'

And Thirkhill enunciated slowly and distinctly the Name of the Holy Trinity.

It was then that I saw the face of the boy Garfield. He did not 'appear,' but he was standing facing us, close by the head of the bed. It was as if he had been there all the while and had now melted on to my vision. The face was distinct, but the figure vague and misty and almost formless. The face had lengthened and thinned and the eyes brightened with a dull sparkle which was not of mirth. I think I was less frightened than amazed. I was standing up, and now I leaned against the wall, with the palms of my hands flattened against it, and stared, motionless. Then Thirkhill's voice spoke again, almost without a tremor.

'Why are you here, Garfield?' he asked, sternly and solemnly. My spirit rather than my ears seemed to hear the answer. It seemed to come from a great distance, very faint, and yet distinct, almost as if a star were speaking on a still night.

'There is nowhere else for me,' the voice said.

It is impossible for me to describe the tone of it, save that it was very simple, very childish, and immeasurably forlorn.

'Why must you be here?'

'I don't know.'

'Why are you always with Peplow?'

'I'm lonely,' said the little, woebegone voice.

'Do you know that you are harming Peplow—making him ill? Why were you with him on the track?'

'I wanted him to win,' said the same childish, almost witless voice.

'Will you always have to stay here?'

'I don't know.'

'You don't want to?'

'Oh, no!'

'Poor Garfield!' murmured Thirkhill, suddenly shaken; and the other voice echoed pitifully:

'Poor Garfield!'

'Can't you leave Peplow alone? You are harming him. And you always liked Peplow, didn't you?'

'I don't—remember. It is all dark. I can only find my way here.'

The words dropped slowly one by one, as with an effort. And in the midst of my blurred emotions of fear and awe and wonder I felt in my heart a great pity for this poor, blind, groping little soul, without understanding, with scant consciousness, almost without memory, compelled by some inscrutable law to wander among the scenes of its earth-life.

There was a long pause, during which I heard Thirkhill fighting to regain his power of speech.

'Garfield,' he said at last, 'you are soon going to be happier. You will not always have to wander here. We are going to ask'

He broke off and slid down upon his knees, and I did the same, covering my eyes with my hands. I do not know what Thirkhill prayed; I only know that I lifted up my heart in one long wordless supplication.

When I uncovered my eyes, we were alone with Peplow, who was quiet now in a calm sleep, and on his lips the faint smile of one who has found peace after pain.

There is little more to tell. As the days passed Peplow grew less and less conscious of the presence of Garfield's spirit, and by the end of the term he was almost his old self again.

But I interviewed his father in town and told him how the death of Garfield had preyed upon his son's mind. I did not tell him any more than that, but I made it plain that I thought the boy required a change. So it came about that Peplow did not return to us after Easter, but went instead to an agricultural college.

He writes to me frequently now, and sometimes mentions what he calls his 'morbid imaginings,' from which he is satisfied that he has now recovered. Well, neither Thirkhill nor I will ever tell him the truth ...

Corner Cottage

We took the cottage for three reasons: because it was cheap, because it was close to the village and shops, and because there was a studio in the garden. It was called Corner Cottage for the obvious reason that it stood upon a corner.

Its exterior was not beautiful, but this had its compensating advantages. It was close to that Mecca of trippers, the Goldney Woods. I have seen as many as ten coaches parked in the village on a summer Sunday, but no strange faces were pressed against the panes of our front windows and no strange voices cried: 'Ooh! Isn't it quaint and picturesque!' Had the people who roamed about like strayed fragments of a flock of sheep known the story attached to our unpretentious residence our weekend peace might have been considerably disturbed. The landlord of The Blue Fox, however, who dispensed beer and shilling teas to these weekend pilgrims was loyal to my expressed wish, and the pilgrims departed with their bags of sweets and nosegays of wildflowers without knowing that our home was the scene of a tragedy which had caused a nine days' wonder and horror.

It is with reluctance that I drag the forlorn tale from its grave, but it is necessary for me to do so, else this story would be no story at all. I had taken the cottage because of the studio and naturally wanted to know who had been my predecessor.

I soon learned that I had several, but local people were reluctant to talk. The Corner Cottage had had many tenants during the past three decades and none of these had stayed very long. Then somebody, less secretive than his neighbours, told me that the cottage had once belonged to Hugh Blaxton—hence the outdoor studio—and that 'it' had happened there. Like myself Blaxton was a black and white artist—if you look in bound volumes of the magazines of a few decades ago you will find plenty of his work—and in his spare time he did some colour work, hence the studio with its skylight in the little garden. I was too young at the time of the tragedy to have heard of it then, but the old hands told me in my Art School days, when little did I think that I should some day come to live in Blaxton's old cottage.

Blaxton was young, ambitious and full of promise. He pulled his fair share out of a 'pool' which in those days was not so great as it is today. He was married to a nice woman and had a charming little daughter of six. For the child he had made a swing in the orchard. When I had the cottage—and to this day for all I know—there were some black strands of rotten rope still fluttering from a bough, like rags caught and hung there by the wind.

One summer evening while Blaxton was out the mother was swinging the child, and probably swung her too high. It is easy to surmise that the little girl felt her hold slipping and cried out for help, and that the mother rushed to try to stop the swing. The swing must have caught the mother full in the forehead—they found the mark upon her afterwards—and the impact caused the child to loose her hold. The child's neck was broken.

Easy to imagine the heart-broken mother staggering back into the cottage with her dead in her arms. When she found that the life which she had given had been taken away she did that which is forbidden by the laws of God and man. She took Blaxton's revolver from the sitting-room mantelpiece and thought to make an end of her own wretchedness. When Blaxton returned he found his dead. There were five live cartridges left; Blaxton needed to use only one of them. The tragic three were found by the charwoman on the following morning.

No wonder the cottage, with so sinister a story in its recent history, was vaguely supposed to be haunted. The number of its tenants and their short tenancies would have been sufficient in any case to start that much hunted hare. Yet the local people did not believe it. It is curious how times have changed. A hundred years ago it was only the bumpkin who believed in supernatural manifestations and was laughed at by his betters. Now only a section of the educated believe in 'ghosts', and it is the bumpkin's turn to laugh. That is what Browning would have called one of Time's Revenges. I must say that I was all with the modern bumpkin when I took Comer Cottage. So was Helen. And Peter, aged nine, believed in nothing less material than the ghastly sweets sold in the village shop. I don't think we were any of us good 'subjects' for a house with such a reputation.

Yet we were plainly expected to do as our immediate predecessors and make a hurried departure. The old maids and retired Service men and their wives—such as constitute the 'cottage gentry' of most English villages—were plainly a little curious as to how we liked our new abode. They remembered so many families who had come to live for years and remained only for weeks. Not that they believed that anything really happened. Oh no! Still, there had been the So-and-so's and the What's-their-names, and the Thingmebobs, who had come to live in our cottage for years and remained only for weeks. Such nice people too, and one wouldn't have believed that they could be so ignorant and superstitious.

I may as well own that I was a customer at the village inn. I spent half an hour or so there on most evenings, gossiping with the local worthies and drinking some very good beer. The people there were plainly wondering how long we should stay. Not that they believed in 'anything funny happening at Comer Cottage'—oh no! But still a lot of ladies and gentlemen—educated ladies and gentlemen too—had come to end their days there and had left in a mere matter of weeks or months.

Villagers are nowadays very shy of being thought 'simple'. When they talked of the 'ghosts' at my cottage I knew that my leg was being gently and politely pulled. There was one exception in old Chudd.

Old Chudd was an ancient rustic who had never shaved in his life. I doubt if he had ever attempted to trim the full beard, whiskers and moustache which had, quite literally, grown white in his service. Winter and summer he wore a bowler hat and an overcoat, both of which had once been black and were now a rather pleasing shade of green. Sometimes he wore a collar without a tie, and sometimes a tie without a collar, as if he had vowed that never the twain should meet.

By occupation he was a hedger and ditcher, his one apparent recreation was the slow consumption of beer. Unless somebody came in who was 'minded' to treat him he could make a pint last all the evening. He spoke little but sat still, apparently 'taking in' all that was going on around him, like an old parrot that was shy of speech.

Generally I bought the old man a drink, which he accepted with a subdued intensity of gratitude, and uttered slow words of goodwill, which sounded like a solemn benediction. One night some of the younger and cheekier had been trying to pull my leg about the reputation of my cottage which had gained me a substantial reduction of rent. I had returned as good as I got, and the youngsters had just deserted me for the dartboard, when I felt the ancient tugging at my coat.

'Ah!' he said. "Tes all right for they to laugh. But yew wait for the spring. Yew wait for the spring, sir.'

'Et tu Brute!' I laughed.

I don't suppose he recognised the last words of the great Caesar, but I think he guessed what they implied.

'Yew wait for the spring, sir.'

In a moment we had changed parts. I was the sceptical Caesar, and he was the soothsayer bidding me beware the Ides of March.

'Yew'll be gone like all the rest of 'em, sir. It was in early March it happened. Yes, yew'll be gone.'

What could I do but laugh?

'Yes, sir, I've seen and 'eard. So will you. And yew'll be gone like all them others. I've seen and 'eard too.'

No more could I get from him. He sat nodding and looking as grave as the old parrot with which I have already compared him. March came in obedience to the call of the calendar, and then the trouble started.

Looking back on this nightmare I can say that it had its parallel with the nightmares which most of us have endured in sleep. It began with a vague uneasiness which grew and grew until the climax.

How did it really begin—and when? I am not quite sure whether or not a vague sense of unrest preceded the slight disturbances at night or vice versa. Somehow I wasn't quite happy. Nor was Helen. Nor, I could see, was Peter. It was as if some slight malaise, too petty to be mentioned, began slowly to affect all of us, and went on gathering a sort of strength or momentum.

The two adjacent bedrooms, occupied respectively by Helen and me and by Peter, were both at the back of the cottage and overlooking the orchard. It was towards the end of February that our troubles began.

What were they? Oh, just nothing at first. Just the ordinary little annoying things that keep people wakeful at night.

First of all there was Peter in the next room getting restless in his sleep and waking up and crying. Then there was a slight but irritating series of noises from the orchard outside—by no means sufficient in themselves to wake one if one were already asleep, but annoying because they were regular and rhythmical.

Creak, creak, creak, creak—a loose bough somewhere caught by the wind. But the creaking went on night after night, wind or no wind. A score of times I must have gone to the window, dreaming of hand-saws on the morrow, and failed precisely to locate the trouble. Sometimes there was no wind at all but the creaking went on just the same. It sounded—well, I hate to say it—like somebody rocking in a swing.

The light of a night sky, however—whether the moon were visible or no—showed me bare and impassive trees, and a waft of breeze never accelerated those strange monotonous sounds.

Creak, creak, creak, creak—I think I shall hear that creaking until I die.

As the nights passed so Peter became more troublesome. I had to get up and bring him into our room. Nor for a time could we find out precisely what ailed him. Like many children of his age he was shy even with his parents.

Then we drew out of him the fact that he 'didn't like the little girl being in his room'.

But for the reasons that Peter would not have understood, and that his mother would have disapproved, I fear I should have made some joke about the outraged proprieties. And then I had a nasty sensation as of a cold knife being drawn through me. The local reputation of our home, the creaking sound in the orchard which was so like the creaking of a swing, and Peter's imaginary little girl—of far less dove-tailed material had ancient legends been made.

It was all nonsense, of course, but the creaking went on night after night, and Peter saw the little girl and ran into our room, and there was a general feeling of 'upset' all day. It was not at all the kind of atmosphere to encourage a poor devil of an artist to get on with his work.

Well, things of that sort—I have studied the subject since—seem to gather a momentum until there comes the crash. There was the story attached to our abode, the creaking in the orchard and Peter's nightmares. The creaking and Peter's cries—followed by his stories of the visitations of the little girl—went on night after night until we had to take him into our room all the time. There he was fairly quiet but still troubled, especially when that branch outside began to creak.

I wish I could convey in words the vague horrors of the nights which followed. So vague were they that if we had tried to express them to others we should have seen only those 'understanding' smiles which are the armour of polite people who cannot possibly understand. Neither Helen nor I would own to the other that each was perfectly aware that something was going on outside normal experience.

It was the same every night—the creaking bough, wind or no wind, the child's restlessness and our own manifest but unmentioned sense of uneasiness.

Then came the unforgettable evening. Why cannot we forget the things we want to forget? Pleasant memories seem to elude one except in moments of happiness. Ugly memories are guests at the board, companions by day and bedfellows by night. This I know will read like the dream of a fever patient. I cannot help it. I can only say that I wish it were. Unhappily for my peace of mind there is corroborative evidence.

That evening I went out after the last meal, and at the risk of having the rest of my tale discredited, I own that I went into the local hostelry. Old Chudd was there and drank the quarter of an inch of beer which remained in his pint glass and looked at me expectantly.

Unless poverty compels I am never able to withstand the mute appeals of dogs and men. I caused his glass to be refilled. He probably respected me about as much as he respected a stone in the road, but he wished me his 'best respects'.

He looked at me curiously over the rim of his pint glass and suddenly put on the air of the soothsayer of ancient Rome. Farcically enough, although he meant to be portentous, he uttered the title of a musical comedy famous a few years ago.

'Tonight's the night,' he said.

I asked him what he meant.

'Up at your 'ouse, sir. You go 'ome and you'll see.'

I took about as much notice of that remark at the time as Caesar took of the incredible bore of a soothsayer who bade him beware the Ides of March. Ten o'clock came and I went home. I let myself in and entered the small apartment which we dignified by the title of drawing-room. To my surprise my wife had company. Also she was as white as a sheet and on the verge of tears. She uttered not a word of greeting, but her look said: 'Oh, I'm so glad you've come!'

The visitors were—well, we will call them a man and a woman. So they looked and so they had once been. All three were around the fire, my wife in the comer and the other two fronting the grate. My wife lifted a distressed face to welcome me. It was a real welcome. In one dreadful shattering moment I was jerked into believing something which I had hitherto held to be incredible.

They were both dressed in the fashion of three or more decades ago. The man wore a stock, the official badge of the artist tribe. The woman wore a pinched waist and puffed-out sleeves. They were not old, but their complexions were that of paper yellowed by age. They were like a pair of dingy waxworks.

Helen, whose eyes were dilated and wild, uttered not one word of greeting or introduction. The man half rose and bowed, the woman inclined her head. I don't know if any responsive civility came from me. I sat down—and was thankful that there happened to be a chair behind me. Both this dreadful pair were disfigured. Each had a little blue-rimmed hole in the forehead, and thin trickles of blood running down. I knew who they were!

We sat in utter silence. Neither the two living nor the two dead made any effort to talk. There was nothing to say. I suppose in some voiceless way I prayed to be relieved of my agony.

The candles were burning very low and keeping a level pace in their race for dissolution. Suddenly one of them fluttered and went out in the rather dreadful way in which one imagines a soul departs from a body.

There was a sudden cry from upstairs.

'Mummy! The little girl! The little girl!'

I saw Helen try to rise. I too tried to lift myself, but I was like a man fainting and yet conscious. Then the flame of the second candle leaped and sank, leaped and sank, and then died, leaving us all in the small light of the fire.

Life came back to my limbs. Somehow I rose and crossed the hearth, brushing, I suppose, the knees of that dreadful couple. I don't mind owning that I went to Helen, fell on my knees before her and buried my face in her lap. One of her arms fell around my shoulders and her face drooped to mine. It was a very cold cheek that I touched, for she had fainted.

I don't know how long we remained like that, clinging together like two frightened children. I don't know how long it was before I dared to look behind me. When at last I collected the remnants of my courage the firelight showed me that the room was empty save for ourselves. Then without a word we went upstairs together to the boy who still cried fitfully.

We left the next day. The hurried departure was highly inconvenient, but we would sooner have slept under a hedge than remained. It was not a dignified retreat, but we did not care. Anything was better than a second encounter with that dreadful couple.

Neither Helen nor I told anybody why we went. I suppose the village people guessed and tongues wagged. In the atmosphere of enlightened Chelsea we still held our peace. Neither of us wanted it to be thought that we were both mad, or one mad and the other lying. It is thankless work to speak of the incredible to the incredulous, and hard to speak of a memory that lingers and troubles like an ever-present ache.

We read of what followed in the local paper sent to us by an old lady with whom Helen remained in correspondence.

The cottage, fortunately empty, caught fire one night. A spark from a passing steam tractor must have caught the thatch. Our old home was a bonfire before the nearest fire brigade could reach it. Had we been there, I suppose—but I hate supposing.

Is there ever an explanation of such things? None in this case which would survive two minutes' cross-examination by a witty counsel in a court of law. To most sane people we are either lying or must thank the great god Coincidence for our escape. People who give credit to no other gods still believe in coincidence.

Yet I like to think that that tragic three somehow managed to return and, with the most benevolent of intentions, to frighten us away. It is a secret which may be revealed to us—not in time but in Eternity.

Meanwhile we go on living—and thinking—and trying to learn.

The Breaking of the Spell

It was my first visit to Rothbridge Hall since Arthur Ferrand's marriage; and I will admit that I went down full of curiosity.

Three months ago Arthur had written to say that he had become a Benedict, and rumour was quick to inform me that the lady of his choice was the daughter of a small local farmer. Ever since then I had been wondering. Arthur was a boy of twenty-three, and, no doubt, desperately in love, but I feared for his future if the local families should refuse to know his wife. The Ferrands had not been long enough in the county to do just as they pleased. I was, therefore, anxious and curious to see how the land lay down at Rothbridge. A man may love his wife to the utmost of his power, and yet grow to hate her if he finds her to be a barrier between himself and his acquaintances. Mere acquaintances are worth nothing as individuals, but as a crowd they help to keep the little devil Boredom at a distance.

But when Arthur met me at the station I knew that all was well. The smile on his face signalled good news to me. He looked foolishly happy, and years younger. He had grown grave and 'stodgy' in his latter 'teens, and now he seemed to have got back all his boyhood.

As we drove the three miles between the station and the Hall he told me that his mother still lived with him. That I accepted at once as a good sign. I had imagined the older Mrs Ferrand living in a continual round of country house visits, lamenting to her various hostesses the dreadful mistake her poor boy had made. That she should still be living with him proved that she had taken her son's wife to her heart.

I found her almost as happy as Arthur, and Mrs Arthur charming She was a mere child of twenty, natural and sweet and jolly. She had no false airs and graces, nor was she unduly timid and shy. She held her place at the head of Arthur's table as if she had been born and bred for the part. I—well, I loved her, and told Arthur so, and he smiled and vowed not to be jealous, because I was only one of many.

There were some people to dinner that night, Lady Bryce-Mannister among them. I wondered, smiling to myself, if Arthur had arranged for her to be there to show me that his wife had made friends with the county. What Lady Bryce-Mannister did other people imitated.

The guests left early, and at about eleven o'clock Arthur's wife and mother both retired, guessing that we should be grateful for a chat in private.

A servant brought in whisky, glasses, and syphons, and left us lounging on either side of the drawing-room fire, grinning contentedly at one another.

We did not speak for quite five minutes, but sat and regarded one another thus. We had been pals for years, and there are some men you can be quite happy with in silence.

I'm glad you're here, you old blighter!' Arthur said at last, I'm jolly glad! Well, tell us what you think. Have I got that worried look which all married men are supposed to acquire?'

'Worried look!' I repeated. 'You lucky, lucky man!'

His grin broadened.

'Yes, I know. I don't know what I've done to deserve it, Billy. All the luck's come my way! Didn't you get a shock when I wrote and told you I was going to be spliced?'

'I was surprised,' I admitted.

'Of course you hadn't even heard of my wife before. You've been such a stranger this last year. She's one of the best, really she is, old man. And she saved my life, Billy, you know.' 'Did she, by Jove!'

'M'm!' He flicked half-an-inch of ash from his cigarette with one of his long slender fingers, and looked deep in the fire. 'And the funny part is she doesn't know. Nobody knows but the mater and I I told the mater. People wouldn't believe; they know too much nowadays. If I thought you wouldn't laugh, Billy'

'Of course I wouldn't laugh!' I promised him.

He sank back in his chair, and was silent for a long while, it's so jolly hard to begin,' he murmured at last. 'I bet you do laugh, Billy; you'll never be able to swallow it! By the way, do you notice anything queer about the room?'

I looked around. The room was just as I had always remembered it.

'Not a picture here that you haven't seen before?'

Then I noticed to what he referred. On the wall to my right hand was the portrait of a young woman, full length, and about half life size. She wore a simple white dress cut in the fashion of the Regency days, and she was strikingly beautiful. Her eyes were curiously expressive for those of a portrait, and I had noticed earlier in the evening that they seemed to follow one about the room. She was not smiling, but looked out of the frame with a fixed intensity. It was not, I could tell, the face of a good woman.

'Why, I have seen that before!' I exclaimed suddenly, it used to be up in the gallery.'

'True!' said Arthur. 'And I had it brought down here—very much against the mater's wishes. I'm not afraid of that girl now, Billy. She can't hurt me!   She's bilked—beaten! Nellie beat her—Nellie, my wife.'

'I should have thought she died years ago,' said I.

'So she did—in 1811.'

I stared at Arthur.

'Old man,' said I, 'you're half asleep, and talking bilge. Better turn in.'

He sat up quickly in his chair.

I'm as wide awake as you are,' he said. 'But I said you'd laugh at me.'

'I won't laugh. Go on.'

There was a short pause. Then he resumed.

'She died in 1811. She was the last of the Gilver family who'd owned the house and estate for about two hundred and eighty years. Proud people they were, and they'd have sold their souls to keep the family from becoming extinct. They simply worshipped the house. This Barbara Gilver—the last of them—was engaged to a man. He was to take the name of Gilver, so as to keep things going. But she died of a fall from her horse a month before the wedding would have taken place. As she lay dying she cursed whatever families should afterwards inhabit the house; she said that the eldest sons would die before they had heirs.'

I looked at the face in the picture, but only for a moment. It was not a nice face, in spite of its beauty.

'After the Gilvers came the Seagolds. Young Seagold, the son and heir, fell into the lake and was drowned at the age of seven. The estate passed over in due course to the Meadings, on the distaff side. Again the young son and heir was killed—climbed on the roof, and fell off.

'Then people began to remember the curse, and the Meadings cleared out. After some years my pater acquired the property. He didn't believe in the curse. He died when I was a kid of about four. Then there was me.'

'But you've survived,' I said

He nodded.

'Yes, I've survived. That's the story I'm going to tell you. I warn you you'll find it queer.'

He lighted another cigarette, and began.

'It's a funny thing, but one of my first memories is that portrait in the gallery. I have the vaguest recollection of my father, but if I hadn't seen that portrait since he died I should remember it quite clearly now. And I didn't like Barbara Gilver's portrait one little bit.

'As a tiny kid I was always begging my nurse to take me up to the picture gallery to see it. It was a sort of treat to me, I don't know why. And I used to love to make faces at it, and put out my tongue. And my nurse used to smack me, and tell me not to be a vulgar little boy. Once, I remember, she told me in a hushed voice that it was a very wicked lady, and might do me harm if I were rude to it. But I don't remember being impressed.

'As a tiny kid I used to miss not having a sister. I don't know who put the idea into my head, but I used to want one, and ask when she was coming. My nurse told me that I might have one some day, doubtless expecting that the mater would marry again. So I was always on the look-out for one, and used to stare curiously at strange little girls, seeing in all of them a possible sister. I had some vague idea that she would not be a baby, but a girl of my own age or perhaps just a little younger.

'At seven my nurse gave place to a governess who never troubled me very much with lessons, and I was allowed to run wild. I had an hour's riding with one of the grooms every morning, and most afternoons I was sent out to play in the garden without much supervision. But there were bounds which I was supposed to respect, and generally did.

'One afternoon, when I was about eight, I was playing by myself in the garden on the lower terrace, behind the tennis courts. I was sitting on the ground, trying to sharpen a home-made arrow with a blunt penknife, when I chanced to look up, and saw a little girl standing still and smiling on me from a few yards away. She looked, as nearly as I can remember, about seven years of age, a queerly dressed kid, and strikingly lovely. Her hair was long and black, and twined with red berries. And there was something vaguely familiar about her face, as if I had once known her, and forgotten her.

'I ran to her and asked if she were my sister. She may or may not have answered, but I know that she accepted the part, for I was mad with joy, and wanted to take her into the house to show her to my mother. But this she seemed not to agree to; she wanted to play out of doors.

'The queer thing is that I can't remember her saying a word. But I knew her meaning just as if she had spoken to me. She wanted to play, and she set off dancing before me, and I followed.

'We got to the little bridge over the stream where the garden ends and the park begins. That was the extreme edge of my bounds, and I hesitated. But she went dancing on over the bridge, and I followed, feeling very naughty. It was then that I began to be afraid of her.

'I think I would have turned back then, but somehow I hadn't the power. I had to follow that queer, graceful, dancing little girl—my new sister—with the berries in her hair. So together we ran across the east comer of the park, she always just in advance.

'There was a gap in the oak fence down in Shallow Lane, and she scrambled through, and I after her. The strange thing is that I went so unwillingly. I was now thoroughly frightened, for I had never before been out of the park except in the company of some grown-up person.

'Lord Notcham's land begins on the other side of Shallow Lane, and soon this queer little girl and I were trespassing. And as we scurried between the trees I kept on hearing a banging noise that added to my fears. 'Presently she burst through a hole in a hedge, and I followed close at her heels. I heard another bang, and a shout, and something seemed to snatch away my sailor hat. The little girl had vanished, and I looked around for her dazedly, wondering where she could have hidden herself. And as I looked, I found myself standing close beside a great target riddled with holes.

'The next I knew was that a man waving a red flag was shouting hoarsely at me and running towards me; and I began to sob, suddenly discovering how near I had been to death. I had strayed on to Lord Notcham's private rifle range, and the local volunteers were practising. 'I remember babbling to the man with the flag about my little sister, but he had not seen the little girl—and neither had the men who were firing—and he knew that I was an only child. They thought my fright had turned me silly for the moment, and carried me home.

'I got a bad scolding, but I did not say a word about the little girl. Somehow I was afraid to, and that was not only because I thought that she too might be scolded. For months I hoped and feared that I might see her again. I used to dream about her, sometimes pleasantly, sometimes horribly. But I did not see her again for what seemed an age of time to a child of my years.

'I was about ten when I saw her next, and that was only for a moment. I was hiding on the cellar stairs to frighten poor old Samson when he went down to bring up some claret. It was dark, but there was just sufficient light to see by. I happened to look down, and there she was, standing at the bottom, smiling up at me.

'She seemed to have grown a little older, just as I had. I don't remember how she was dressed, but her hair was longer and fell over both shoulders, and there were no berries in it. As I saw her I forgot that she had nearly been the cause of my death. I was delighted to see her, and felt that I loved her.

' "Hullo!" I cried, and waving my arms I came dashing down the cellar stairs.

'I had reached the last step before I noticed the open well at the bottom. How I escaped falling in, Heaven knows. By instinct I jumped and cleared the well, and as I stood trembling on the further side I looked around for her. She was not there.

'Again, I said nothing to my mother, except that I had nearly fallen down the well. There was a row about it, but we never found out who had left it uncovered. By that time I had of course given up the idea that this strange little girl was my sister, and I began to wonder and worry about her identity.

'For weeks and months after that I used to spend long hours thinking about her. I loved, feared, hated her, all at the same time. It was evident that she wanted to kill me, and I could not think why. What harm had I ever done her? It wasn't fair that she should hate me when I loved her so. I didn't know in those days the difference between my childish affection and the hypnotic spell that the little ghost-girl could weave around me at the first glance of her eyes.

'Twice she had tried to kill me, and twice she had failed. I wondered if she would try again, and used to give myself some bad times by thinking about it. But eighteen months passed before I saw her again.

'I had gone to a prep, school, and was on my holidays. The mater had taken me to Cripton, a jolly little place on the East Coast. Two or three of the kids from my school were stopping there, and that gave me extra liberty. I was already more boy than child, a pretty lively sort of kid, not at all the kind that sees ghosts. Young Dorritty was stopping there—you probably know him, because he came on to Wryvem afterwards and got into the eleven five years ago.

'Well, young Dorritty and I used to play cricket on the downs above the high cliffs; and one afternoon we had a row. I had swiped the ball over the cliff, and as the tide was up it was lost for good and all. It was Dorritty's ball, and he slanged me for hitting so hard. I said it was his fault for bowling me a half-volley. One thing led to another and ended in a fight. I was pretty useful, but Dorritty was a heavier kid, and I took my gruel from him I bubbled like a two-year old with pain and shame, and young Dorritty picked up his bat and stumps and walked off whistling, leaving me curled up on the ground. 'I lay there a long time, for I dared not go home with my traces of blows and tears. I suppose I thought I shouldn't be allowed to play with young Dorritty anymore. And strangely enough I still wanted to, and didn't bear him a bit of malice. You know what kids are.

'Then she came.

'I was wild with fear when she bent over me and I saw who it was. But it only lasted for a moment. The next, I loved her so that I would have followed her through the gates of Death—as I very nearly did.

'Again I don't remember that she spoke, but she put her arms around me and laid her face against mine. She was so sorry that I had been hurt! And although I knew my danger I felt that the licking I had had was worth while for the sake of the amends she made. Again she had grown a little older and bigger, apparently keeping pace with me in age. And again she reminded me of someone—someone I had known for a long time.

'Presently she sprang up like a little nymph and I followed. I had forgotten all about the danger of her companionship. I had forgotten about the close proximity of the cliffs, and followed her blindly until suddenly I found myself hurtling through space.

'But once again she had failed. I fell only a dozen feet or so and tumbled, hands and knees first, on to a broad ledge of the sandy stuff that the cliff was composed of. I managed to climb up, dirty, frightened and battered, and made my way back to the hotel. That made three times—and three times I had been saved in some miraculous fashion!'

'Good Lord, Arthur!' I broke out at last.

He threw away his cigarette and lighted another, staring at me all the while.

'Wait a little,' he said. 'There is more to come!'

'I didn't see her again until after I had met you. I suppose about five years had elapsed. I was nearly seventeen then, and at Wryvem.

'You might remember that night, but you weren't in my house. It was just after Gray resigned and Sartley took over the house. You know what an old fool he was, and how the chaps hated him. He kept on putting the fellows' backs up. The limit was reached when he forbade us to drink cider. You'd remember the row there was because all the chaps turned up at one call-over wearing bits of blue ribbon?

'Only about four or five chaps used to drink cider before Sartley made a fuss. After that everybody did. We had a cute way of getting it into the house, which Sartley never found out in my time.

'We used to drink it in the bedrooms at night, and some chaps may have liked it, but I could never stand the beastly, sickly, stuff. It never stood the least chance of getting into anybody's head, although I've seen some fellows blow themselves out with it.

'How we used to manage was like this: It was pretty easy to break bounds from any of the windows at the back. There was an easy drop on to the roof of the boot-room, and another easy drop to the ground. We used to have the cider hidden in a certain spot in that ditch that runs along outside the cricket ground. Covered over with dock leaves nobody was ever likely to see it. Then one of us would get out at night and go and fetch it.

'One night it was my turn, and it was just one of the most perfect nights I've ever seen. There was a lovely clear sky, a crescent moon, all the stars burning like candles, and a nice warm breeze carrying along the smell of flowers from the house garden. I never was a poetical sort of kid, but a night like that couldn't fail to stir me.

'When I got outside I felt light at heart and skittish as a colt. I didn't want to get back to the stuffy four-bedded room. Then I thought it would be rather a lark to stop out for a good while and give the other chaps a fright—make them think I'd been caught. So I went on to the cricket field and walked round the boundary towards the pavilion.

'When I had gone a little way I found that I was not alone on the field. At the first sight of the figure that advanced towards me I ducked, and would have run. Then I saw, however, that it was a girl and not a master. I wondered who it could be, and waited.

'She came towards me quite fearlessly, and my heart began to beat. I wasn't such a kid but that a moonlight meeting with some nice girl had its attractions for me. So presently I called out: "Hullo, who is it?"

'She swerved away, with a musical little laugh. As nearly as I could judge she was a girl of sixteen or seventeen. I laughed, too, and ran after her.

'I didn't quite catch her. When she was within arm's length of me she glanced at me over her shoulder, showing her teeth in a broad smile. Then I knew her, and my heart turned to water. She was the bogie of my childhood, whom I had begun to disbelieve in, almost grown up, and come for me again. And one other thing I saw in that quick turn of her head—I knew who she was. The maturity which her face and figure were beginning to develop showed her extreme likeness to the girl in the portrait at home; and I knew that she was the spirit of Barbara Gilver.

'In a flash I remembered the story of the curse, and I knew the reason of this awful visitation. I realised my danger with a queer tingling sensation in my nostrils. And all the while that queer love of her was in my heart—that extraordinary impulse that bade me follow when she beckoned. 'This time I tried not to go, but the effort was wasted. I was like a man being carried along by a relentless current, with nothing to cling to. In a vague way I searched my mind for something to cling to—something to tell me that I needn't follow her. But I did follow her. I had to!

'She danced along as of old, always just beyond my reach, like the ideal in an allegorical picture. Presently I found myself climbing one of those old oak trees the fellows often used to climb. Looking back I can remember that there was nothing ungraceful in her climbing. It seemed to be as natural in her as in a squirrel. And my one idea by that time was to catch her—though I don't know why—and when she got to the top I was sure that she couldn't escape. We must have been forty or fifty feet in the air when she climbed out along a great branch which was bare of twigs and foliage. I followed her and, suddenly as a snap of the fingers, I found myself alone. I had not time to be surprised, because the branch snapped under me. It was dead!' For the first time during his strange narrative I saw an expression of horror on Arthur's face. It had happened so recently as to be still vivid in his memory. He paused and brushed his forehead with his handkerchief.

'I fell,' he said slowly, 'and landed on a branch about six feet beneath. I carry the scar of my scraped shin to this day. I fell plumb and balanced—just well enough balanced to give me time to get hold on the sound branch, cling there, and recover myself. Then, somehow, I clambered down.

'That was the last time I saw the spirit of Barbara Gilver until a few months ago.'

He paused again—paused for so long that I found my voice and prompted him.

'And then?' I said.

He looked up.

'I'm going to tell you. The last time, did I say? Well, perhaps not quite. About three years ago I dreamt of her. "Next time!" she whispered. And I was quite certain that the next time I saw her would mark the day of my death. I could not expect another miracle to save me. And yet it was, I suppose, a kind of miracle—the sort of miracle we don't believe in because we see it every day. A good woman's love is a kind of miracle, Billy!

'Of course, you don't know how Nellie and I met and conducted our courtship. She had just the proper amount of pride, and wasn't going to play the beggar maid to my King Cophetua. She gave me a thousand heartaches before I won her. Then we used to meet sometimes in the copse by Rowan's farm. It had to be done that way until I'd won the mater over.

'One evening I was waiting for Nellie, not too certain that she would come. It was already dark, but the moon was up, and the shadows of the trees and bushes made a sort of lattice-work across the paths.

'Suddenly the bushes parted half-a-dozen yards away from me, and a face looked out. Barbara Gilver had come again!

'But this time I could feel no insane desire to go to her. I felt only fear and loathing. I was attracted to her, as before, just as if she had been a magnet and I a needle, but none of that strange sisterly affection crept in to drown my fear.

'I took a step towards her, and managed to stop. She beckoned again imperiously, and I took another step, but very slowly. Hard as it was to resist her, it was easier than it had been before. I was still the drowning man being hurried along by the rapid current, but now there was something to cling to! I loved Nellie. I had her love to cling to. It seemed to give me strength to keep my distance from this vile apparition that had once had full power over me.

'The Thing went on beckoning, and her smile became uglier. She came towards me, and then edged away again. I suffered physical fatigue, as if I were engaged in a tug-of-war with some stronger and heavier opponent. How long it lasted, Heaven only knows!

'Then I heard a quick step behind me, and the next moment Nellie was in my arms. And, looking over her shoulder, I watched the defeated soul of Barbara Gilver slink away into the bushes, and fade, and vanish. But before she went I saw an awful change come over her face—age, and malignant hate, and dreadful agony. That night, Billy, I swear that I saw a lost soul in all its naked horror!

'I trembled all over as I kissed Nellie. She didn't understand when I told her she had saved my life. But she had; and henceforth I shall be safe, Billy, so long as I keep her love. I shall have something to cling to—something to cling to so that I needn't go when Barbara Gilver beckons!'

He paused, and threw away the end of his cigarette.

'That's the story,' he said in a changed voice, 'and there's the portrait of Barbara Gilver. I had it brought down here because I'm not afraid of her. A whim of mine—a bit of bravado. Now, Billy, say, am I a liar?'

What could I tell him? But if it were a lie it is the first one he has ever told. And if it were a lie it is an unconscious one—a lie he believes implicitly.

A.M. Burrage – The Life And Times.

Alfred McLelland Burrage, better known as simply AM Burrage, was born in Hillingdon, Middlesex on July 1st, 1889, to Alfred Sherrington Burrage and Mary E. Burrage. On his Father's side writing already ran in the family's blood as both he and an uncle, Edwin Harcourt Burrage, were writers of the then very popular boys' magazine fiction.

Life in late Victorian times was by no means easy and writing has always been a precarious career for most. For an insight into the young AM and his surroundings it is interesting to see how certain facts were captured in the 1891 census when he was aged one. The family is listed as living at Uxbridge Common in Hillingdon. His father is 40 and his mother 36. In the next census of 1901, and with it the end of the Victorian era, the family has moved to 1 Park Villa, Newbury. In that time his father has aged 17 years his mother 6 years and young AM has disappeared from the records. It's almost a precursor to one of his stories.

There is little documented about his growing up and education. What we can glean though is something about his environment. His neighbours were varied: a tailor's journeyman, a corn porter, a lodging-house keeper and a grocer's assistant. Nothing particularly illustrious, so times cannot have been as rosy as they should, especially in the light of his Father's hard work. Alfred Sherrington wrote for The Boy's World, Our Boys' Paper, The Boys of England, and various others. He also appears to have written under the pseudonym Philander Jackson and edited The Boys' Standard and that one of his more celebrated pieces was a retelling of the story of Sweeney Todd entitled "The String of Peals; or, Passages from the Life of Sweeney Todd, the Demon Barber".

Sadly Alfred Sherrington Burrage died in 1906. There is a biographical note in Lloyd's Magazine, from 1921, which suggests that young Alfred McLelland was studying at St. Augustine's, the Catholic Foundation School in Ramsgate, and most probably away from home at the time.

A.M. Burrage was 16 years old when he had his first story published; the same year as his father's death, in the prestigious boys' paper, Chums. It was a great start to his professional career and whether doors had been opened by his father and family or not the young man's career now had to stand on its own. He was now primary provider for the household and this was the only way he could do it. His Mother, sister and aunt must be provided for.

Magazine fiction was his family's blood and business and for A. M. Burrage, business was good. He established himself as a competent and creative writer and was busy writing stories and articles on a weekly basis for publications such as Boys' Friend Weekly, Boys' Herald, Comic Life, Vanguard, Dreadnought, Triumph Library Cheer Boys Cheer, and Gem, under the pseudonym 'Cooee'.

However, unlike his father and uncle who had remained firmly and easily categorised as boys' writers, he had his sights set on the more well regarded, more lucrative, adult market. Burrage was aided in his early years as a professional writer by Isobel Thorne of the off-Fleet Street publishing firm Shurey's. Her publications have been characterised as "low in price, modest in payments, but whose readers were avid for romance, thrills, sensation, strong characterisation and neat plotting", and this estimation of her publications also fits nicely the description of Burrage's own writing at that time. For a young writer this sort of readership was vital, and the modest wages he received were bolstered by the exposure the publications brought him. Burrage was certainly helped by Thorne's use of young writers.

At the time Burrage was beginning to really establish himself as a writer, the entire magazine fiction scene was benefiting from what we would now see as disruptive influences: new printing techniques, a growing readership with more disposable income and leisure time and other media failing to provide – though obviously movies and such were only in their infancy at the time. The market was lively and commercial, and the readership interested, excitable and willing to pay. P. G. Wodehouse, of Jeeves fame, recalls these years:

We might get turned down by the Strand, but there was always the hope of landing with Nash's, the Story-teller, the London, the Royal, the Red, the Yellow, Cassell's, the New, the Novel, the Grand, the Pall Mall, and the Windsor, not to mention Blackwood's, Cornhill, Chambers's and probably about a dozen more I've forgotten.

With War clouds darkening the skies of Europe in 1914 Burrage was firmly established as a magazine writer, securing publication in London Magazine and The Storyteller, which were both highly prestigious publications. Alongside he had plenty printed in less illustrious publications such as Short Stories Illustrated.

By now Burrage, a young man of twenty-four-year-was eligible for the Armed Services. Under the 'Derby Scheme' he confirmed that he was available for service if called upon in December 1915. Conscription was to follow shortly though, by that time, Burrage had already voluntarily enrolled in the Artists Rifles.

The significance of Burrage's decision to join the Artists Rifles is made clear by the nature of the unit itself. They formed in the middle of the nineteenth century, a group of volunteer artists comprising musicians, writers, painters and engravers. Minerva and Mars were their patrons, one of wisdom, arts, and defence, the other of war. The unit boasted several significant figures as ex-servicemen, including Dante Gabriel Rossetti, Algernon Charles Swinburne and William Morris. It was a popular unit with students and recent postgraduates, and the training was considered and extensive.

In Burrage's vivid, celebrated account of World War I entitled War is War, he insists that he was a volunteer and not a conscript, though as has already been noted, it is quite possible that his decision to join such a respected territorial unit may have been more of an effort to secure himself a more congenial army posting; had he waited for conscription, he would have had little choice over those with whom he was posted. Unlike poets Wilfred Owen or Edward Thomas, Burrage did not achieve a commission, and he suggests in War is War that this may be a result of his extremely unmilitary personality and his shortcomings as a soldier.

Add to this the fact that as the breadwinner for the family he was putting himself in harm's way. If anything were to happen to him the result on the family would be devastating. With the death of
Edwin Harcourt Burrage in 1916 it came even more starkly into focus.

Even though he was now a soldier he was still a writer and writers had to write. It also helped that it was a distraction from the mindless carnage around him. He experimented with various genres, excelling in the one that was to prove most lucrative for him; the light romance, in which a male character invariably meets a female character, there is a problem or hurdle to their being together, they overcome it and they live happily ever after. Burrage's talent for this formula was such that he could work seemingly endless minor variations from the same basic storyline and so he was able to keep writing a steady body of easy work.

He gives a fascinating account of the practicalities of writing such fiction during wartime in War is War, in which he remarks on the difficulties of censorship: "the problem of censorship was an acute one to me. It was well enough to write a story, but the difficulty was to get it censored. Officers were shy of tackling five thousand words or so, written in indelible pencil..." After some time he managed to find a chaplain who was willing to undertake the censorship. However, in order to secure this chaplain's favour and thus his services he was obliged to appear to be holy. Though he did so in earnest while he was with the chaplain, his efforts were dashed when the chaplain found him, sprawled on top of a young girl, and realised Burrage's piety to be a fraudulent con. As Burrage had anticipated, the reality of his behaviour ensured that this particular opportunity was swiftly ended. Resourceful to the last, though, he writes of his solution: "there were 'green envelopes' which could be sent away sealed and were liable only to censorship at the base, but these were only sparingly issued... I met an A.S.C. lorry driver who had stolen enough green envelopes to last me for the rest of the war; and since he only wanted two francs for them I was free of the censorship from that day forward."

Although we know that Burrage had his family to support at home as an incentive to keep writing, at times in War is War he reveals a more intimate aspect of his relationship with his work.

"It was a great relief to me to write when it was at all possible – to sit down and lose myself in that pleasant old world I used to know and pretend to myself that there never had been a war. Some of my editors seemed of the opinion that we were not suffering from one now. One used to write to me saying "Couldn't you let me have one of your light, charming love stories of country house life by next Thursday." I would get these letters in the trenches during the usual 'morning hate' when my fingers were too numb to hold a pencil, when I was worn out with work and sleeplessness, and when I was extremely doubtful if there ever would be another Thursday".

Writing is a useful therapy and for Burrage it provided a means to escape if only for a short time to a world that he could control and move at will.   With the misery and harsh conditions of the War dragging on he was eventually invalided and so he returned to England.

One of the best insights we have as to the character which Burrage presented on his return from the war is to be found in Lloyd's's 1920 publication of Captain Dorry, one of Burrage's story series. In that publication there was included a brief sketch of Burrage, describing his personality.

A.M. BURRAGE is the type of young man who might very well walk out of one of his own stories. He commenced yarn-spinning as a boy of fifteen at St Augustine's, Ramsgate, writing stories of school life to provide himself with pocket-money. Since then he has won his spurs as one of the most popular of magazine writers. Everything he does has charm and reflects his own romantic spirit – for he is incurably romantic and hopelessly lazy. It is his misfortune, although he would not admit it, that his work finds a too ready market. Nevertheless, his friends hope that one day he will wake up and do justice to himself. Otherwise he may end up as a "best-seller", a fate which doubtless he contemplates with equanimity.

Despite the sketch's fairly accurate but negative summation of Burrage's literary output up to that point, some of his stories seem to exhibit a desire to write about more than just his usual romantic plots. The most immediate change of this nature is in his decision to bring some of his wartime experience into his work, despite being perfectly aware that such writing was not at all what his editors desired, for they feared it would upset and intimidate their readership.

An example of this can be found in "A Town of Memories", published in 1919 in Grand Magazine, in which he uses his well rehearsed romantic story with a slight shift of emphasis to explore his own return from the war and the general reception which soldiers received on their return. Following a young officer as he returns to the town in which he grew up, Burrage portrays an almost hostile environment into which he returns; he is unrecognised, and nobody pays any interest, respect or attention to him or his stories of the war, nor even to his reception of the Distinguished Service Order. Instead, the people of the town have their own interests and priorities with which to concern themselves. Though this contentious portrayal of post-war society certainly marks a slight shift in Burrage's writing, he returns to the romantic convention expected of him by reuniting the officer with a beautiful girl who had admired him throughout school.   It would be harsh to not accept that market conditions expected one thing and to ignore them would mean turning his back on publications who still clamoured for his penmanship.

Another of Burrage's alternative directions is to be found in "The Recurring Tragedy", in which a General whose war tactics of attrition had been to the slaughtered cost of his soldiers, and he comes to re-imagine his own past as a Judas figure in a terrible vision. The Strange Career of Captain Dorry became a series for Lloyd's Magazine in 1920 about a gentleman crook and an ex-officer with a Military Cross who, idle in peacetime, meets a mysterious man called Fewgin whose business is in stolen goods and mind reading. Fewgin realises Dorry is a suitable candidate for recruitment into his gang of like-minded ex-military thieves, stealing only from "certain vampires who made money out of the war, and, by keeping up prices, are continuing to make money out of the peace". Again, in this motive, we see a glimpse of Burrage's own feelings on the war, as there is undoubtedly a bitterness towards those profiting from the suffering of others in such a manner. Fewgin justifies himself, saying:

"I help brave men who cannot help themselves. I give them a chance to get back a little of their own from the men who battened and fattened on them, who helped to starve their dependents while they were fighting, who smoked fat cigars in the haunts of their betters, and hoped the war might never end."

Burrage began to see slightly more success in the 1920s, achieving a couple of hard back publications entitled Some Ghost Stories and Poor Dear Esme. The latter, a comedy, concerns a boy who, for various reasons, is forced to disguise himself as a girl. Though these hard cover publications were a notable achievement, and one of which he was proud, the fact was that there was less money in it than in the magazines. In his history of the Strand Magazine, Reginald Pound portrays Burrage around this time, likening him to his equally prolific contemporary Herbert Shaw, considering them "two Bohemian temperaments that suffused and at times confused gifts from which more was expected than come forth. They had a precise knowledge of the popular short story as the product of calculated design. Both privately despised it, though it was their living."

The early 1920s, and with them a boom in prosperity, hope and happiness, now brought with them an increase in demand for war stories. Rather than preferring to ignore the atrocities of the war, which had seemed the general attitude in the immediate post-war years, society became more interested and concerned with the manner in which the war was fought, and the greed and political battles which had necessitated such bloodshed. Burrage answered this demand in 1930 with his own epochal piece, War Is War. He published under the pseudonym 'Ex-Private X', saying "were it otherwise I could not tell the truth about myself", though its publisher, Victor Gollancz, "who published the book and greatly admired it, had to point out that the critics would hardly take the book seriously if it became known that the author earned his living producing two or three slushy love stories a week".

In one of a series of letters he wrote to his contemporary and fellow writer Dorothy Sayers, Burrage bemoans how War is War "promised to be a great success, but was only a moderate one". The book itself was received with reviews on both sides of the spectrum. Cyril Fall's War Books, a survey of post-war writing published in 1930, gives a clear indication as to why the critics were so mixed in reception of the book. He writes:

This book is extremely uneven in quality. The account of the attack at Paschendaele and of conditions at Cambrai after the great German counter-attack are very good indeed; in fact among the best of their kind. But the rest is disfigured by an unreasoned and unpleasant attack on superiors and all troops other than those of the front line, which is all the more astonishing because the author is inclined to harp upon his social position as compared with that of many of the officers with whom he came in contact. He does not use as much bad language as many writers on the War, but his methods of abuse will leave on some of his readers at least a worse impression than the most highly-spiced language.

Dorothy Sayers was the editor at Victor Gollanz for anthologies of ghost and horror stories which included stories by Burrage. She says, in one of her letters of Burrage's story The Waxwork, a piece beyond the nerves of the editors, "what you say about "The Waxwork" sounds very exciting, just the sort of thing I want. Our nerves are stronger than those of the editors of periodicals, and we will publish anything, so long as it does not bring us into conflict with the Home Secretary". Though their correspondence began as strictly business, Burrage's acquaintance with Atherton Fleming, Sayers's husband, allowed their interactions to become less formal and friendlier. Burrage wrote of Fleming "I hope to encounter him soon in one of the Fleet Street tea-shops". 'Tea-shop' being a popular euphemism for the pub, where both Burrage and Fleming could frequently be found, though their alcohol consumption came to damage both their health and their professions, with Burrage coming off the worse.

Happily for Burrage, as a result of being featured in one of Sayers's anthologies, The Waxwork became one of his best-known stories and it would grab the attention of the film companies several times down the years even becoming an episode in the TV series 'Alfred Hitchcock Presents'.

The developing friendship between Burrage and Sayers enabled him to reveal more details of his personal life, admitting to her his "neuritis at both ends (legs and eyes)", and hinting at his troubles with alcohol: "Fleet Street is not a good place for a man who delights in succumbing to temptation, and whose doctor says that even small doses of alcohol are poison to him". Sayers sympathises, replying that Fleming "agrees with you entirely about the temptations of Fleet Street; he has, however, succeeded, through sheer strength of character, in being able to drink soda-water in the face of all his fellow journalists".

In another of Burrage's letters, he apologises for a delay in sending proofs of a story, with the words:

I have had a pretty thin time lately through illness and anxiety. And for days on end haven't had the energy in me to write a letter, and when I had the energy to send a complete set of proofs to you I found I hadn't the postage money (This is when you take out your handkerchief and start sobbing). I owed my late agent over £1000, so I got practically nothing out of War is War. He stuck to it. Well, he is paid off now, and so are my arrears of income tax. All this took a toll of my very small earning capacity, and I have been sold up. This on top of something which promised to be a great success and was only a moderate one, was a bit too much for me. Still, in spite of sickness I am resilient and shall float again. "You can't keep a good man down," as the whale said about Jonah.

For a man who had so many stories in so many magazines, and was gaining pace in Sayers's anthologies as a talented writer of horror stories, his income will have been far higher than the then average wage, and yet as he says, he finds himself short of money.

Several questions are left unanswered about his personal life. It is unclear whether he was still supporting family, or whether he spent the majority of his money on alcohol, or whether he chose to conceal his true fortunes from those around him. Perhaps most incongruous is the apparent absence of a wife; though his death certificate indicates that he had one, listed as H.A. Burrage, he seems never to mention her to Sayers.

He was around forty-two when he wrote that apology letter to Sayers, though in tone and circumstance it seems to be from a man in a far later stage of his life.

Burrage continued writing until his death in 1956, and continued to be prolifically published. Indeed, the Evening News alone published some forty of his stories between 1950-56. His death is recorded at Edgware General Hospital on 18th December, and the causes of his death are recorded as congestive cardiac failure, arteriosclerosis and chronic bronchitis. He was sixty-seven years old, and his last address is listed as 105 Vaughan Road, Harrow.

Though his name is not often remembered in lists of prominent writers of his time, or even it's genres, his ghost stories are highly regarded by critics and fans alike, while his life story tells us much about the trials and stresses placed on authors during and after the war, and on soldiers returning from that war. His reluctant acceptance that the money was in the magazines while the esteem was in the poorly-paying hard covers, and his persistence as a writer, speak of a determined man, doomed to circumstance yet living as best he could.

In ending A.M Burrage wrote a few sentences which best sum up two things. Firstly his love for his son Simon (who sadly passed away in October 2013 and was a great and passionate advocate for his Father's works.) and secondly his succinct reasons for writing.

TO JULIAN SIMON FIELD BURRAGE
who at the moment of writing will
soon achieve the great age of four.
From somebody who loves him.

In War is War I admitted being a professional writer, or in other words one who depends for his bread and cheese and beer on writing, typing or dictating strings of sentences which his masters, the Public, are kind enough to buy and presumably to read.

The book brought me letters from a few old friends and a great many new ones. A large percentage of the new friends, who missed having seen that my identity was rather unkindly betrayed by the Press, wrote and asked (a) who I was and (b) what sort of stories did I write?

The answer to the second question will be found in the following pages. The answer to the first question is 'Nobody Much', worse luck.

Most of these stories were written with the intention of giving the reader a pleasant shudder, in the hope that he will take a lighted candle to bed with him—for candle-makers must be considered in these hard times. Some have already made their bow from the pages of the monthly magazines. The best have, quite naturally, been rejected.

www.ingramcontent.com/pod-product-compliance
Lightning Source LLC
Chambersburg PA
CBHW071008280626

47160CB00015B/2064